Sweet Matchmaker

Indigo Bay Sweet Romance Series
Book 2

Jean Oram

Oram Productions Alberta, Canada

This is a work of fiction and all characters, organizations, places, events, and incidents appearing in this novel are products of the author's active imagination or are used in a fictitious manner. Any resemblance to actual people, alive or dead, as well as any resemblance to events or locales is coincidental and, truly, a little bit cool.

Printed in the United States of America unless otherwise stated on the last page of this book. Published by Oram Productions Alberta, Canada.

LIBRARY OF CONGRESS CATALOGING-IN-PUBLICATION DATA

Oram, Jean.
    Sweet Matchmaker: Indigo Bay Sweet Romance Series / Jean Oram.—
    1st. ed.
        p. cm.
    ISBN 978-1-928198-39-0 (paperback)
    Ebook ISBN 978-1-928198-31-4
1. Romance fiction. 2. Romance fiction—Small towns. 3. Small towns—Fiction. 4. Indigo Bay (Imaginary place)—Fiction. 5. Interpersonal relations—Fiction. 6. Undercover operations—Fiction. 7. FICTION / suspense. 8. FICTION / Espionage. 9. Romance fiction, American. 10. Marriage—Fiction. 11. Man-woman relationships—Fiction. 12. Romances. 13. FICTION / Romance / Contemporary. I. Title.

First Oram Productions Edition: May 2017

Cover design by Najla Qamber Designs
Www.najlaqamberdesigns.com

Dedication

To my readers. For everything.

Acknowledgments

I had a blast writing Ginger and Logan's story and I hope my readers absolutely adore them as much as I do. The six of us authors had a ton of fun writing the Indigo Bay world for you, our readers.

A special thank you also goes to the team who help me write the best story I can; Margaret, Emily, Erin, Lucy, Rachel, Donna, and Mrs. X. I'd also like to thank fans Lenda Burns and Jaime Deming for helping me name Logan Stone. You rock, ladies!

As well, a big thank you to my fans for patiently waiting for me to get back to your favorite characters from Blueberry Springs—I hope you enjoy this Indigo Bay adventure!

And finally, thank you to my husband for stocking up on frozen pizzas so those nights when I didn't have any dinner ideas after sitting in at my computer writing all day I still looked like a hero to our kids. XO.

Happy reading,
Jean Oram

Sweet Matchmaker

CHAPTER 1

Logan Stone pulled the ill-gotten invitation from the breast pocket of his sports jacket. One small fib and he would be through the doors and into the party for engaged couples. Then he could be on the lookout for Vito Hart, diamond smuggler. Vito had been working the week's events here in Indigo Bay, hobnobbing with people like Logan, a wholesaler of loose diamonds. Little did Vito know that Logan had plans to put him behind bars before he could ruin any more happily ever afters with bad deals and violence.

Logan had been deep undercover and without agency resources for six long months while tracking Vito, edging closer and closer. And now, as a (fake) wholesaler for a (fake) international business, he was almost in. Almost had enough incriminating intel to put the man securely behind bars and stop one nice chunk of the illegal trade of conflict diamonds that supported violent rebel forces stirring up civil war and intertribal conflict in Africa.

But three days. That was all Logan had left on his visa before it was game over for his cover and he was deported by the local officers of the law. They'd been tracking him ever since they'd found him with a soon-to-expire visa lurking around Becker's visa and passport forgeries near the docks during one of their sting operations. Not his best day in the field and so much for plan B.

Logan inhaled the mild South Carolina ocean breeze, letting it wash over him as he reminded himself who he was supposed to be—just a wholesaler wanting to get close to a diamond source, as well as potential new clients. He had his name tag, a small brochure, fake business cards and even a simple diamond engagement ring with a spiral Celtic knot design. All part of the shtick. All intended to get him closer to Vito. Bust him before the local officers ejected Logan from the country on Wednesday.

The doors to the event were open, the music pouring outside. In line, engaged couples kissed and held hands, and Logan looked away, not wanting to be reminded of all he'd lost by being selfish so many years ago. He had a job to do today. Nothing more.

He toyed with the invitation while the line slowly moved forward. Get close to Vito, gain his trust. That's what he had to do tonight. The man knew what line of work he was in, though he acted as if he barely knew him. Logan felt Vito needed just one more small thing before he took him into his trusted inner circle.

But what was that missing piece?

Laughter from inside caused Logan to glance up. Vito was near the doors, his wife at his side. Logan had mentioned in passing that he was engaged, but he'd yet to show up with a woman on his arm. Was that the issue? If so, he was going to have to find a civilian, seeing as it was too risky to break his silence with HQ and ask for a female field agent to come play the part. There was a good reason he had gone silent—Vito was no dummy and likely had more than the one guy Logan had noticed sporadically keeping tabs on him.

Which meant it was time to finally show up with a fiancée.

Logan needed to regroup before he saw the smuggler again. Turning on his heel, he left the line, nearly bumping into a woman in a clingy green dress that brought out the spark in her matching eyes, the fiery highlights in her auburn hair.

"Oh! I'm sorry," she said.

"My fault. Are you all right?"

Her smile grew as she nodded. "Australian?"

"That I am, mate." He laid his accent on thick and her grin took on a hint of slyness. The sheila liked accents. And he liked her. She had the kind of curves and smile that had him taking a second look back as he made his way down to the beach.

Hot, that's what that woman was. If he hadn't been on a mission he'd be trying to spend a little time with her. And since he *was* on mission, he should be doing the same, to use her to further his cover. But civilian covers were tricky. Risky.

Logan walked down to the Atlantic, letting the sound of the crashing waves fill his mind.

He was tired. Unenthusiastic about maintaining his cover, managing a million lies. He stared out at a blinking buoy marking a shoal, and rolled his shoulders. Maybe it was time for a new job. One with more toys, more excitement.

Yeah, he had toys and occasionally even got to use them. And as for excitement? His work was either deadly boring or so exciting he nearly died. Literally.

He needed something in between, like his agent friend Zach Forrester had been talking about—private security.

That would be nice. Lots of toys and the kind of excitement that didn't get him killed.

Just about perfect.

He also wouldn't have to worry about his next mission taking him away from Annabelle Babkins, daughter of a fellow agent who'd been killed in the line of duty. Eighteen years old now, Annabelle had a room in an assisted living facility, but her only guardian and advocate was Logan.

Frustration still stirring within him, he began walking back to the party.

Wednesday—that's when it would all fall apart. Three short days.

He'd worked with tighter timelines and knew that when plans continued to fail like they had with this mission, something better was typically lining up for him.

And if not, well, then he'd tag out and someone else would come in and try to get close. But in the meantime, Logan would go old-school and find a nice sheila to lure into a marriage of convenience to help get his visa extended so he didn't get deported. Plan C, because seriously? Nobody at HQ seemed to have noticed that, due to the way Vito kept going dark and the case kept getting extended, Logan's visa was now set to expire.

That meant it was time for him to focus on looking out for number one—himself—and find a lovely woman to marry him.

"BUT I HAVE AN INVITATION." Ginger McGinty waved the printed square of white card stock that was supposed to guarantee entry into the engaged couples event. She wasn't actually engaged—that would have helped solve her money problems, as well as removed her need to sneak into the party. Six months ago her grandmother, Wanda, had offered her a standing deal when they'd drawn up the purchase papers for her bridal shop. Wanda had liked Ginger's boyfriend of the time, Matias, and had told her that if she married him—and stayed with him for a year—Wanda would give her 30 percent off the store's market value. Basically, the amount Ginger had to go into debt for in order to make the purchase and what her grandmother thought would finally inspire Ginger to settle down.

But Wanda, as brilliant as she was, didn't understand. Men left Ginger. It wasn't the other way around. And as Ginger had predicted, Matias had left a few months later. Picked up his bags and moved back to sunny Argentina.

Wanda was a romantic who had enjoyed forty-seven years of bliss with her husband. She'd helped hundreds, if not thousands, of brides fulfill their happily ever afters, after marrying the rancher next door as per her family's wishes. What had been friendship between them had developed into a very loving, strong marriage. The kind that made Ginger wish someone would set her up with someone once and for all. Her grandfather had doted on his wife and supported her dream of opening a wedding shop in the small town of Blueberry Springs. He'd stood by her side and had helped the store grow, right up until his passing a few years ago.

Love like that—as much as Ginger wished for it—just didn't happen these days. People expected too much, weren't honest enough.

Herself included, when it came to expectations. She

expected men to stay. And they didn't. That meant she was single and had to not only pay full market value for her grandmother's successful store, but also needed to sneak into this party for market research purposes. She wanted to find out what made engaged couples chose a particular bridal shop, so she could boost her sales and maybe finally move into a real apartment that wasn't a modified storeroom over the salesroom. That and pay the stifling increase in business taxes the current mayor, Barry Lunn, had slapped on her shop—as well as other town businesses—in hopes of helping their dying little town.

"Where's your fiancé?" the man at the door asked, barring her from entering.

Ginger glanced at his name tag. He was young and wore the surfer persona well. "Kelso, he'll be here momentarily," she said, trying to act as formal as he was. She had an invitation. Who cared if her imaginary fiancé was with her or not? She had gathered up every last bit of credit she had to make this business trip a reality. The workshops had been great, but she wanted into the resort's parties sponsored by Hart Diamonds.

"You're welcome to wait at the Tiki Hut until he arrives." The man gestured to a thatch-roofed bar down on the beach.

"But I said I would meet him in there."

"How will he get in if you're already inside with the invitation?"

Nuts.

"You'll, um, know him by my description? He's—he's tall. And um...you know? Handsome." She really sucked at lying. How had her father and all her ex-boyfriends managed to do it so often and so well? She silently begged Kelso to let her in.

She decided on a different approach. "Are you engaged, Kelso?"

He shook his head, his bleach-blond hair flopping over his eyes.

"Dating anyone?"

He shook his head again.

"Well then...you know how it feels to be left out of so many things that couples get to do, just because you haven't found the right person yet." Ugh. She was really reaching, as well as pretty much saying she didn't have a man to go with her invitation.

Kelso's hand shifted to the red rope that served as a barrier between her and her research subjects.

Please, please!

"You know the bartender down at the Tiki Hut is single?" she said quickly, when he didn't unlatch the rope. "Vicky? She's cute. Likes to surf and sail. She's totally looking for someone."

Kelso gave Ginger an intrigued look as a man nudged him out of the way, relieving him from duty.

Nuts again!

Ginger turned to the new arrival. "Hi! Kelso and I were just chatting. I have an invitation." She waved it and smiled as she stepped toward the rope.

The new man glanced down at her left hand and she casually slipped it behind her back, hoping he hadn't seen that she lacked a ring.

It was unfair to keep single people out. Unjust! At this rate, she was not going to recommend Hart Diamonds to the brides who came into her store.

She tried for a smile as Kelso filled his replacement in on

her lack of a present-and-accounted-for fiancé. "I promise to be good."

"That's not the first time I've heard you make that promise," said a playful, deep voice with an Australian accent. A large hand landed gently on her shoulder, filling her with warmth. She turned to see the man she'd bumped into earlier smiling down at her.

She lost the ability to form words as she took him in once again. He was gorgeous, his demeanor oozing masculinity and power. His gray eyes were playful and serious at the same time, with a hint of trouble. Fun trouble.

"Were you waiting long?" he asked, playing the concerned lover.

She was still without words. He was pretending to be her fiancé. He was trying to help her get into the party.

He was her hero.

Well, that might be a bit overboard, but he was something, that was for sure.

"I'm sorry I'm late, honey," he added.

Honey.

Oh, what she wouldn't give to hear that every morning for the rest of her life. The man was huge. Hot. And his sexy Aussie accent, a favorite of hers, was doing squishy things to her knees. And his body...it was like he lifted Mack trucks as part of his regular workout. His shoulders were so broad she could imagine him carrying their kids on them.

She straightened. No. No more romances. No more men with accents who weren't permanent residents. Men lied. Men left. She was done with that. She was off the market for anything more serious than flirting. Her home and business were here, on this continent.

Her bridal shop. That's what she needed to focus on. She'd been saving up for it since she was sixteen, and it was her chance to fulfill happily ever afters for others. She'd been raised in a small town full of matchmakers, and the fact that she was still single at the ripe old age of thirty-one meant one thing: she wasn't marriage material and it was her destiny to help others find happiness. Help brides.

The Australian was watching her with amusement, sending a fizzy feeling through her bloodstream. No, she was not going to move across the world for a man—not even him, as cute as he was, and as perfect as his timing seemed to be.

But she *was* willing to pretend to be his fiancée so they could enter the party.

She turned to the men at the door with a large smile. Her grandma had said to come play, have fun and live a little. It was her time. And Wanda was always right.

Well, most of the time.

Ginger slipped her arm around the waist of the man beside her. Massive. He was absolutely *massive,* and radiated warmth and virility in a way that made it difficult to breathe.

Wow.

"Here he is," she said weakly. She was going to have to buy herself a fan if she spent any time around this dark-haired hunk.

She gave her head a shake. Not spending time. Just getting across the threshold.

Threshold. He could totally carry her over it without straining his back or breaking a sweat.

Party threshold. Double wow. Her mind was zipping around like a caffeinated squirrel on a hunt for hidden nuts.

Kelso smiled and opened the red rope. "To the lovely couple."

"Thank you. And totally ask Vicky out," Ginger said as she passed.

"Right on," he replied.

As Ginger's fake fiancé followed her in, she heard Kelso say, "Buy your woman a ring, dude."

"Just got it back from sizing, which is why I'm late," the man said mildly.

Her Aussie was quick with the right words, that was for sure. She probably would've made something up about swollen fingers, and then been found out when the bouncer looked at her slender, unpuffy hands.

Then again, maybe the Aussie sucked at lying, too, because he'd just implied he had a ring for her.

"That's what they all say," Kelso muttered.

"What did you expect me to say? It's gone walkabout?"

"Kinda."

The rope clicked into place behind them and a waiter in a tuxedo came by with a tray of wine. Ginger took a glass and grinned.

She was inside!

Everywhere, partygoers mingled, chatting and laughing. The outer walls of the ballroom were lined with bright booths where wedding vendors were offering giveaways, balloons, flowers, and promoting everything a couple might need for their wedding day. Formal wear to catering to honeymoons. Everyone was so happy, so alive. There were so many people she could chat with. Where was her list? She opened her clutch, trying to pull out her notepad, while keeping her glass upright. She'd been attending wedding workshops for two days now, brainstorming ideas, and was eager to ask real-life brides-to-be what they wanted most in stores like hers. Did they want to be able to get tuxes as well as their dress? What type of accessories? Did they want a newsletter with sales notices? Inspirational ideas posted on social media? Recommendations and discounts for things like invitations and cakes? So many questions, so many possibilities. Ginger didn't even know where to start. She began to approach a large group, but then someone grabbed her elbow.

She turned, worried she'd been busted.

Oh, right. Her fake fiancé, Hottie McHot Stuff.

"I'm Logan Stone."

"Ginger McGinty. Thanks for helping me get in."

"It's best to come right after shift change and say your other half just headed inside, while you went to retrieve something. Then point and wave at a random stranger near the door. When they wave back out of politeness, you're in like a wallaby."

"Clever." Ginger reassessed McHottie. "You crash events often?"

He gave a shrug, his expression aloof. "I think it's rather sexist that you have to have a man to get in, don't you?"

"Oh, I see what you're doing."

"What's that?" He looked amused, and Ginger felt that special, intoxicating blend of I-found-someone-new-and-interesting-and-there-could-be-potential-here flow through her. She loved that about foreigners with accents. They always gave her that rush.

"Trying to distract me from your misdeeds."

He gave her a half smile. He was watching the room now, not her. Losing interest, in other words. Story. Of. Her. Life.

"But I understand why they didn't let me in," she whispered.

"Why's that?"

"I look as though I'm about to cause trouble."

His focus returned to her. "You're a sheila looking to cause disturbances by pretending you're betrothed? Bloody sinister. They should lock you away immediately." He pretended to wave to one of the security guards, but she batted his hand down.

"Shh!"

He grinned and took a sip of his wine, watching her. She toyed with her own glass, studying him. He was dreamy and had an edge to him that suggested danger. And that accent?

Yeah, he was completely off-limits.

But she could flirt with him, have a little fun without getting involved—because he was surely a man with one foot already out the door.

"You have a very sexy accent."

"That's all that you've noticed?" He lifted one brow in question.

Oh, he was such flirt.

"Some women go for good shoulders." She studied his over the rim of her glass. "I go for an accent."

He drifted closer, that heat she'd felt earlier radiating toward her again.

"Would you like me to read poetry to you?" he asked, lowering his voice.

Killer accent—and he was using it to make her knees turn to jelly as he played along.

"I prefer rap lyrics."

Logan laughed, his head falling back, his whole body

shaking. She had the feeling she'd taken him by surprise, and it was empowering. She often felt like a small-town nobody who'd gone nowhere and done nothing. Men like Logan were intriguing, and just thinking that she had what it took to make him laugh and snag his attention made her glow inside.

"Logan, how long are you in town?"

"I'M AROUND UNTIL WEDNESDAY morning—my visa expires and I'll be heading back Down Under."

Logan kept one eye on the redhead at his side and the other on the lookout for Vito.

"That's too bad." Ginger's sunny smile flipped into a frown. "Friday's couples event is supposed to be superb."

"You want to keep me as your fiancé until then, do you?"

She gave him a playful look, the sunniness returning almost full-force. "I might have to marry you. Are you handy around the house?"

He blinked, surprised by her joke. Could it be that easy? And yet he didn't think he caught a whiff of truth in her words. She was too bubbly, flirtatious. Smart. She was only kidding, testing him to see what he might be up for this week.

He placed a hand on the wall behind her, leaning closer. "My skills are unprecedented. In every room of the house."

She blushed, her smile growing, open and real. But she didn't take him too seriously, didn't believe there was any validity to his hidden offer.

"You enjoy adventure?" he asked.

"With the right man, maybe," she answered coyly.

"Shall I buy you a ring?" he asked, probing to find out

where she might draw the line. Despite her flirtiness and being okay with a little truth-bending to sneak into a party, he didn't believe she would go along with anything that would land him a visa by Wednesday. She lacked that undercurrent of desperation he needed, and had a perceptiveness that could definitely blow his cover.

He scanned the room again, looking for other possibilities, women who reeked of need, or a wish for the kind of excitement that came with a whirlwind romance and subsequent marriage. Maybe the blonde across the room in the barely-there dress, handing out wedding cake coupons? She had that wistful look, as if she'd been unlucky in love often enough that she might be susceptible to his charms, especially if he flashed some cash.

He'd try her, but it was always best to have a backup plan, as well. He kept searching the businesswomen working the party, hoping another one would stand out as a possible plan B.

"It sounds like you already have," Ginger said.

"Sorry?" Logan tried to focus on the pretty woman in front of him. Her gaze was as captivating as her mouth. Her lips soft and perfect for kissing.

"It sounds like you've already got a ring?" She was referring to the comment he'd made to the doorman on the way in.

"Oh, right."

"Something simple, I hope. I'm not a fancy gal." She was teasing, had noticed his distraction.

To his left he saw Vito watching him with Ginger.

"You don't have a real fiancé or boyfriend hiding somewhere with a shotgun, do you?" Logan asked.

"Sure." She flicked one of his shirt buttons with a finger. "Twelve gauge. We don't mess around in the mountain town where I'm from."

He found himself chuckling, enjoying her repartee. Continuing to play-act her fiancé would be fun for however long it lasted. Five minutes, five days. But he needed more than flirting and a little ruse. He needed marriage.

"Is this your lovely fiancée, Logan?" Vito Hart asked in a smooth voice, joining them. "The beautiful woman I've heard about?"

Shoot. He opened his mouth to deflect the man away, but Ginger stuck out her hand with a smile. "Yes, it's a pleasure to meet you. I'm Ginger McGinty."

Well, it looked like Logan was locked in. Ginger was officially part of his cover and he'd have to find a way to make it work and keep her safe without it all blowing up on him.

He wondered which agent he'd get the tag-in teasing from once he failed his mission, handing it off to someone else.

"Vito Hart, and the pleasure is all mine." Vito kissed Ginger's hand and she bit back a pleased smile. She was a romantic, all right—which could work in Logan's favor. He wondered what she did for a living and how she'd managed to stay single all these years.

"*The* Vito Hart?" she asked.

"The one and only."

"Brides have been talking about your diamonds in my bridal shop."

"Smart women."

Ginger might not realize it, but she was buttering up Vito, making Logan's case so much easier. He began to think that maybe she could work out, after all.

"This wonderful woman has not nearly enough diamonds, Logan." Vito lightly touched one of Ginger's bare earlobes and Logan felt a protective surge zip through him. "You being a wholesaler, I would think your chosen wife-to-be should be dripping in them."

Ginger turned to Logan with a wide smile. "I happen to agree with Mr. Hart."

"Call me Vito."

Logan put an arm around Ginger, half to demonstrate that she was his and half to try and hide her bare left ring finger. Vito was correct; Ginger bare of jewelry did not look the part of his fiancée.

Vito gave them a small smile. "Do come for a day trip on my yacht on Thursday. I'm having some guests aboard as we sail around Kiawah Island. It would be a pleasure to have you both join us and indulge in some R & R out in the sun."

"Oh!" Ginger pressed into Logan's side, soft and distracting. "Can we?"

His instinct was to say yes, boost her smile into one of those big ones he'd already come to adore. He would bet anything that Vito's trip would include clandestine meetings away from on-land prying eyes and ears. He'd likely try to woo a few unsuspecting businesspeople who wanted to make a little extra profit and would accept bulk diamonds, not questioning their origins.

Logan needed to be on that boat. But he also really needed to keep Ginger away from any immediate danger.

"Please?" Ginger asked softly.

He nodded, figuring he'd find a way to leave her safely ashore if he was still in the U.S. come Thursday. Ginger beamed at Vito, giving Logan a boost of pleasure for giving her what she wanted.

"We'll be there."

"Fantastic. And congratulations on your engagement," Vito said, stepping back into the crowd to schmooze with other possible clients.

"That's so nice of him," Ginger said.

Only last year Vito had instigated a bloody raid that had left African villages decimated as he stirred up civil war so he could slip in undetected and steal diamonds from restricted areas, smuggling them off the continent. And now he was planning to sell them, which was where Logan came in. Vito was savvy, but Logan was patient. He'd been renting an Indigo Bay cottage for months, keeping one eye on Vito's beach house and one on the marina where the smuggler docked his yacht. Logan had been listening to feeds from the devices he'd planted, waiting for Vito to reappear, while making himself known as a man in need of diamonds. Lots of diamonds.

The trap was laid.

"I've never been on a yacht before," Ginger said. "Oh no!"

"Thursday," Logan said. "I know."

That was going to be a problem.

"You'll be gone." Her hand was resting against his chest, her expression crestfallen.

"Maybe we can figure something out."

"I hope so."

"Would you like to enter our giveaway?" a woman asked from a nearby booth.

Ginger began chatting with her, then filled out an entry

form, before moving on through the crowds, adding her
name to every door prize draw she came across.

"I love giveaways," she said, when Logan caught up with
her again. "I never treat myself, and the chance of getting a
little gift just for writing my name down tickles me to no
end."

"You're entering to win—" he glanced at the poster on the
side of the box "—an elopement wedding here in Indigo Bay
this week?"

She'd just dropped in her entry form, and paused, reading
the blurb. She shrugged. "I never win anything."

He hoped not. That could get...convenient, actually. If, say,
she needed a groom in the next day or two and he was still in
her sights.

OKAY, GINGER NEEDED TO GET herself back under
control. She was going wild. But all these trips and wedding
accessories just waiting for her to win them? Yes, there were
at least a hundred other entries in most of the boxes, but the
idea that she might win something had her heart racing.
She'd had so little growing up, and since the age of sixteen
had saved every extra penny either for college or so she could
buy her grandmother's store. Even now she couldn't actually
afford this business trip and was worried her credit card was
going to bounce when she tried to check out on Saturday.

She never treated herself. Never did anything as exotic or
exciting as being invited aboard a yacht. She hoped Logan
found a way to stick around so she could go. Plus he was fun.
And cute. Terribly cute.

No, handsome. Much too tall, dark and handsome to be cute.

And that flicker of sadness in his gray eyes? Killer. She wanted to smooth it all away despite his tough and ruthless look.

And yes, she had been joking about marrying him so he could stick around, but he knew that. He had an intelligence that seemed to capture everything, considering each and every spoken word as if it held extra meaning. Total aphrodisiac. Not many men listened like that.

Gullible. She was a sitting duck, awaiting the charms of a man like him.

No more. She'd promised herself to give up her romantic daydreams of being swept away.

Oh, but he was so much fun and there were so many events they could get into this week if they stuck together. He wasn't smarmy or clingy, and she instinctively knew she could trust him. He was someone she could finally let loose with. Like a breath of fresh air. Like a roller coaster taking her to the edge.

And she wouldn't fall for him, because he was leaving in a few days.

It was perfect.

"Can I get you a drink?" Logan asked. She'd left her glass at one of the booths where she'd been entering a draw. She couldn't believe she'd put in her name to win a free elopement wedding. But she loved the idea of a little pampering, some extras she'd never buy for herself.

Although maybe not the wedding.

They made their way through the crowds of laughing people, heading toward the bar at the back of the room. As

Ginger passed chatting couples she realized she still hadn't picked the brains of anyone around her, distracted as she was by Logan and the giveaways.

She opened her clutch, wondering how she could casually hand out a few business cards, and whether anyone would actually order a dress online, sight unseen, since her shop was thousands of miles away.

She closed her clutch, knowing she had to dream bigger to widen her store's reach. She needed something like an in-house designer. Maybe her old college roommate, Olivia Carrington, was looking to get out of public relations and back into designing.

"Where are you from?" Logan asked. He had one hand pressed lightly to her lower back as he guided her between clumps of partygoers, sweeping her aside when a waiter just about backed into her.

She could get used to that. His warmth. Having someone at her side looking out for her.

Okay, so she was lonely. Forgive her. She worked in a wedding store and was single. The whole "I'll be happy for everyone else" really wasn't working for her, no matter how hard she tried to convince herself otherwise.

But she was moving on. Flings, not relationships.

No more heartbreak. Her bad spell had started with Kurt, her high school sweetheart, and it hadn't stopped, right on up to Matias from Argentina.

Her new motto: Be Flirty. Have Fun.

Don't Fall in Love.

"I'm from Blueberry Springs, which is in the Rockies," she said, answering Logan's question, "I'm an Aquarius. And you?"

"I'm from Australia and I have no idea what my sign is. And before you ask, no, I don't live near Uluru—Ayers Rock."

"Totally a Leo. No, Taurus," she amended. "When's your birthday?" She detected a bullheaded stubbornness within him. A commitment to ideas, which she quite liked.

He passed her a glass of chardonnay and smiled at someone behind her. She turned to look. Oh, dear. It was Ted Tremblay, a tall, scrawny fellow engaged to Nadia Forsee, who was not only gorgeous, but smart. A sweet couple from Arizona, they had been in a few wedding biz workshops with Ginger over the past two days. They owned a large chain of jewelry stores and were looking to expand their market.

Logan immediately pulled Ginger to his side, and she wished he'd give up the charade, because this was going to get sticky. Even if she did find herself wishing he'd snuggle closer.

"Logan, Ginger! I didn't know you two were engaged." Ted was smiling at them as if he'd just discovered the secret to world peace.

"You know Ginger?" Logan asked. "She totally swept me away."

Logan gave her a wink that warmed her right down to the tips of her toes. Ah, yes. He *was* a little naughty something, wasn't he?

She rested a hand against his chest, not wanting to deceive her new friends, but knowing they would find it amusing when she told them the lengths she'd gone to in order to sneak in and do some market research—assuming she ever got around to it. She glanced over her shoulder, thinking maybe she could discreetly whisper something to Nadia. But the bartender was watching them as if he suspected they were indeed gate-crashers and not legitimate guests.

"He actually ran me over like an unleashed dog," she said, smiling at Nadia and Ted. "Nearly knocked me right off my high heels."

Logan laughed, the sound again making her think he didn't do it very often. It made her want to make him laugh more. "I have that effect on women."

"I can't believe you didn't tell me!" Nadia's gaze went straight to Ginger's finger.

Ring? Absent. Yup. That was going to be a problem by the end of the night, wasn't it?

"Oh," Logan said, digging through his sports jacket's inner pocket. He'd seen Nadia's look and was up to something. When he pulled out a ring box Ginger knew their game had suddenly gone too far.

"I was getting it sized," Logan said. "I'm a wholesaler, but I know a guy who does some gem setting and he did a quick resize for us this afternoon." He smiled and opened the box.

Ginger felt her eyes drawn to the object shining on its bed of blue velvet. She'd never been offered an engagement ring before. Not even by Kurt, who had sworn he loved her to the ends of the earth—which apparently didn't include a college located on the other side of the continent, seeing as he'd stayed in Blueberry Springs and married one of her distant cousins instead of coming with her.

Ginger found her hands moving toward the box of their own volition. The ring was perfect. A Celtic design with emeralds and diamonds, and intricate knots woven around them. She knew she should stop the lie, step back. Because what man carried an engagement ring in his pocket and pretended to be engaged to a stranger?

Well, he was in jewelry. It was likely a sample or something. But still. This felt...too much.

"Oh, look at your face," Nadia said. "They're so sweet, Ted." The two cuddled, watching the fairy tale unfold.

Logan was angling closer, like he was ready to grab Ginger if she decided to start running.

She looked up at him and he brought his mouth close to her ear, acting as though he was whispering sweet nothings. "It's just a sample I carry around, Ginge."

He'd shortened her name. Given her a nickname. That hardly felt fair.

"If you don't want to play along, just blink twice and I'll get us out of here," he said. "But if you want to have some fun with it, I'm your man, and you can borrow the ring for as long as you need. I know what it's like, trying to get deals in this business when you're single. People think you're some kind of fraud."

There was an honesty in his expression, a glint of sadness that she identified with. She knew what he was talking about. It was like she was a fake for selling wedding dreams to others when she was basically a few cats and a deck of cards away from being a card-carrying spinster. The jokes and ribbing never ceased; the silence was never anything but awkward when new brides asked her about what her own big day had been like.

Logan stepped back, and she found the warm box in her grasp. He handed the couple his business card, telling them if they needed anything to let him know, deflecting their attention, giving her a moment to decide.

How had Ginger's father lied so successfully for all those years? Telling her and her mother that he loved them and couldn't imagine life without them? Although maybe that part was true, and a big part of why he'd kept his other woman a secret. He knew Ginger's mom would flip out and carve him from their lives once she found out—which she did. She had been completely fooled, and ultimately decimated. She'd believed she was part of a happy, solid couple who watched football on Friday nights, played bridge with their friends on Tuesdays. They practically kept the plastic on the couch, their lives and relationship were so perfect and clean.

And it had all been a big lie.

Just like Ginger's last boyfriend, who'd stuck around mostly in hopes of her sharing her health plan with him. Her grandmother had thought he was The One, but Ginger realized now he'd just needed more time before he took off. And yet she'd still managed to convince herself that it was real, thinking he'd give her a ring like this one.

She was unlucky in love because she was a big, romantic, gullible sucker, and men could sense it.

She pushed the ring onto her finger. It fit perfectly. What did that mean? Was it some sort of good omen?

No, she was thinking about it all too much. It was simply a game. And what happened in Vegas stayed in Vegas, and because she lived so far away from the Carolinas, she figured the same applied here. It was her turn to have some harmless fun, her turn to use a man and get what she wanted.

And she wanted to have fun, wanted into these exclusive events, wanted to be taken seriously by the vendors she'd spoken to this week. She wanted to take her business to the next level, and this would help her.

Yes, it was lying to Ted and Nadia, but they'd understand when she told them in tomorrow morning's workshop.

Logan noticed the ring and lifted her hand, a strange look on his face, as though he might be remembering something from the past. He met her eyes and gave a nod. "It suits you."

"You have good taste."

"I claimed *you*, didn't I?"

Oh, she only wished that were true. "You say the best things, Logan."

"It comes naturally when I'm around you."

Ah, he had a romantic streak, it seemed. The kind she'd seen only in movies or read about in books, and it made her heart beat a little faster.

"Did you run some of your store activity ideas by all these brides-to-be?" Nadia asked. So far she'd been one of the best for brainstorming with.

"I haven't had a chance," Ginger replied.

"He's been keeping you busy, I imagine," the woman said, giving her a nudge in the ribs.

Ginger opened her mouth. What could she say?

"Ginger McGinty!" bellowed a voice, and there on stage was a tall man in a pale suit, smiling out at the crowd. "Ginger McGinty, you've won two tickets to the Southern hospitality dinner, which includes an evening of entertainment and more!"

Ginger placed a hand over her chest. "I won! I never win," she breathed.

Could this be another big three? On her way to the workshops her first flight had been cancelled. Her rental car had had a flat tire before she'd even made it out of the lot, and her room in the economy motel hadn't been ready upon her arrival.

That was three not-so-great things.

But then three definitely great things had happened. The airline had given her a free meal and set her up on the next available flight, which had been direct, getting her in half an hour earlier than the first one. The car company had upgraded her to a convertible, and the Indigo Bay motel had set her up in her own cottage along the ocean for no extra charge.

She was a strong believer in the power of three, and tonight things were coming up on the lucky side of it. First Logan getting her into the party. The yacht invitation. Now this.

She flung her arms around Logan and he lifted her off the ground. He felt strong and somehow familiar—a man she could get used to.

He released her and she turned back to the stage, uncertain if she was expected to go up there to claim her prize.

"Go! Before they give it away to the next person," Nadia said, her hands on Ginger's back as she pressed her forward. She stopped pushing Ginger and hauled on Logan's arm. "Logan? Get up there!"

Ginger looked back to find Logan following, his eyes on the stage, his brow furrowed. Then his eyes met hers and his expression softened and she felt it. That special feeling between her and a man. The feeling she'd always been waiting for, curious whether it truly existed.

She gave herself a scolding. She was being ridiculous. It

was just all the love and romance around her that was setting her heart and mind on fire.

Logan was leaving for Australia in a matter of days.

That's all she had to remember. Tonight was about being playful and finding joy, pushing the envelope without any real consequences. She could say anything, do anything, and it didn't matter.

Logan fitted himself beside her on stage as she accepted the prize and she whispered, "You seem to be my lucky charm, Logan."

"And you mine."

He smiled at her and the feeling of being connected blossomed in her stomach, spreading until it filled her. She felt complete, the epitome of life. "I guess in order to secure your ongoing luck..." she paused to bat her lashes at him "...you'll just have to marry me, Logan Stone."

CHAPTER 2

Under the bright lights of the stage, the ring on Ginger's finger flashed, as bright as the woman's eyes. Logan liked her, and he knew it wouldn't be difficult to pretend he was a smitten, happily engaged man if he could convince her to continue along with their "relationship."

The ring flashed again, taking him back in time to how he'd felt once before, when he'd brought his new wife, city born and bred, home to the family's cattle station—a ranch—deep in the outback. Kristy had loved the idea of marrying a man who mustered cattle for a living right up until the moment she realized the truth: it wasn't romantic. Neither was living with a stockman who had to ride out for days, checking on his stock. He'd seen the change in her perception right there, in the cracks in her expression. She'd felt deceived by her husband, who would come home exhausted and grimy after mending fences in the stockyard in the late summer heat, leaving a ring of dirt in the shower—which he'd clean out himself. It wasn't what she'd signed up for.

He'd been selfish, telling her that since he'd gone to the effort of moving back, he was staying. He'd tried to coax her into loving the land, seeing the beauty of being away from a bustling city. But the fact was he'd been selfish, putting his wishes above hers, and she'd done the only thing she could to ensure her happiness—left.

By then his parents were gone, the homestead and surrounding land solely his, seeing as Kristy didn't even want her half. After a long month alone in the sprawling house, he'd sold it all and joined the army, hoping a few tours of duty would work out some of his selfishness.

He still wasn't sure if that had been successful or not. He thought it may have merely morphed his selfishness into ruthlessness.

Logan snapped to the present, to find Ginger McGinty teasing him about securing his luck through marrying her, those cheery green eyes sparkling. He mindlessly clapped as more winners were announced.

It was time to play international spy and hate himself later.

"I'd love to have you all to myself," he whispered. He lowered his lips to hers, drawing out a slow kiss that was innocent, yet not. He'd used The Kiss on many, but none had made him feel the need to slide his arms around his target, pull her body flush with his and consume her with something deeper, much more...intimate and real.

Realizing he was losing control of the moment, he jerked away.

Don't get involved while on a case.

Ginger tumbled into him, her hands splayed against his chest. "Do that again." Her eyes were dreamy, her smile soft and trusting.

Against his inner wisdom, he did.

This woman was a dangerous distraction, but the only one who could help him get what he needed.

GINGER HAD NEVER BEEN KISSED off her feet before, but she swore if there had been somewhere soft to land—like, say, a bed—she would have been sprawled across it from that heady kiss.

Wowzers.

"Who are you?" she murmured against Logan's lips.

"I can't remember," he said. His eyes kept dancing from her lips to her eyes.

The emcee was still pulling more winning names for giveaways, and Ginger realized she should probably drop the bedroom act and behave, since she was still onstage, with gold-and-white balloon columns on either side of her and Logan.

"We were going to hold a vote for the most-in-love couple tonight," the emcee said, "but I think we already found them. Dallas, will you join me for awarding the winners with their prize?"

The owner of the cottages, Dallas Harper, a man in his thirties, hurried onto the stage, all smiles. "Indigo Bay Cottages is pleased to announce that the winning couple of an upgraded honeymoon cottage—and all expenses paid for the week—are these two young lovebirds, Ginger and Logan! Congratulations."

Ginger blinked and laughed. Dallas held out his arms to showcase her and Logan as the audience went wild, clapping and cheering.

Honeymoon cottage? Things had officially slipped from slightly crazy to insane.

She began shaking her head. "No, no. I'm sure..."

Talking her way into a party, accepting a yachting invitation and winning a free supper was one thing, but accepting a honeymoon suite...

And that was more than three. But maybe she was counting things incorrectly. It was now two surprise bonuses and two wins. Which meant the power of three didn't apply today, or there was more in store. Possibly more than she could handle.

"There must be others who could use this prize," Logan suggested.

"Sure, there are many," Dallas agreed. "But that kiss?" Beside him, the emcee shook his hand as if it had been burned, and Ginger had to bite her bottom lip to prevent herself from grinning like a fool. It *had* been a pretty amazing kiss.

"Can we hear it again for our winners?" the emcee called out to the guests. They responded, causing Ginger to laugh with embarrassment. Logan was definitely making her evening memorable.

"There seem to be a lot of perks to being with you," he whispered in her ear.

"And you don't even know the half of them."

Confetti and balloons fell from the ceiling above and she laughed again, hands extended to catch the shiny, glittery squares.

This was amazing. She felt like she was a sweepstakes winner or in a reality TV show.

"We'll have our staff move your belongings from your existing cottages into your new, one-bedroom honeymoon cottage, complete with our complimentary butler service,"

Dallas said. "This also includes a free breakfast service courtesy of my mother's cafe, Sweet Caroline's."

One-bedroom cottage.

Whoa. Wait. What? No-o-o. As hot as McHunky Hunk-Hunk was, staying in a one-bedroom cottage with him had danger written all over it. Sure, having free accommodation might mean she could actually afford to stay right up until the end of the workshops. And, yes, she might be ready to let loose and have a little fun, play a few games with McHottie. But playing house with him in a secluded cottage designed to encourage romance, she might be unable to resist the powers of his accent, and could wind up doing something stupid, like... Best not to think of that while up onstage, with people staring at her, in case she started drooling.

"Look at her! She's stunned by Indigo Bay Cottages' generosity."

Ginger mindlessly started clapping, trying to cover her shock. How were they going to get out of this one? And why now, of all days, was she winning things—things for engaged couples?

Plus a honeymoon cottage brought to life the illicit whisper inside her that suggested maybe she could have what her grandmother, Wanda, had had—a marriage that had been set up by others, but turned out to be the strongest partnership Ginger had ever seen.

But this was reality. Ginger's reality.

The people in charge were pulling entries from a bin for more door prizes, and she continued to clap and smile as more winners joined them onstage.

They'd find a way out of this. Logan was a complete

stranger to her, but surely this made him just as uncomfortable as it did her.

"And..." The emcee was laughing. "This is so fitting! The winner of our elopement wedding is..."

No.

Things happened in threes.

Ginger turned to Logan, who looked as though he was about to burst into laughter.

"Ginger and Logan! Our most-in-love couple. They'll be getting married here this week."

"Oh, I..." Ginger held out a hand to stop the man, while Logan pumped his fist jubilantly. He was really getting into the act.

"You're engaged, aren't you?" the emcee whispered. "You entered and signed."

Ginger glanced at Logan, who was showboating for the audience.

The emcee turned his back as Ginger tried to protest that she really hadn't meant to enter that one, and that they needed a bit of time to sort things out.

Beside her, Logan was laughing, looking immensely amused.

"We aren't claiming that one," she whispered. She shouldn't claim any of it. It was all based on a lie. "This is karma for lying, isn't it?"

He laughed even harder.

"What's so funny?"

"If you like me, just say so—you don't have to rearrange my life."

"Oh, I'll rearrange something if you keep laughing."

He slung an arm around her shoulders, still chuckling. He

lowered his mouth to her ear, his breath hot and distracting, as he said, "We'll figure it out, Ginger. I promise."

LOGAN HAD HAD A FEW GLASSES of wine and was feeling happy. Not so much as to inhibit his ability to do his job, but enough that he could relax, act as though he was a carefree guy around the charming Ginger, convince her he was worth keeping for a while.

He was finally close to locking up Vito. So close he could practically see the red ink stamping the word *completed* across the front of Vito's case folder.

Logan unlocked the honeymoon cottage for Ginger and stepped aside to let his lucky charm head in. With every mission, something presented itself as a talisman, usually meaning the case was about to be cracked in a significant way, and this mission had yet to have one. Until Ginger.

She was standing on the threshold in her green dress, her strawberry-blond curls moving like a curtain in the cool ocean breeze.

While he waited for her to step inside, Logan took in their new location. The cottage was on the grassy dunes overlooking the Atlantic, and had a great view of the surrounding area, as well as Vito's private beach house, a half mile away. This was a perfect place to hide in plain sight while he worked on cracking the case.

"It's even pink on the inside," Ginger said.

Logan turned back to the cottage, which had heart wreaths hanging on the clapboard walls. His fiancée looked disappointed and he peeked over her shoulder. The place was indeed pink, although more pastel with pink highlights, unlike the bright pink exterior. He thought it was actually rather nice, and it had the things a gal might want—fresh flowers, chocolates and a bottle of bubbly chilling in a bucket. From his vantage point he could see the cottage had one bedroom, a kitchen, sitting area and a bathroom he bet included a Jacuzzi tub.

Not two bedrooms, like many of the others stretched out along the beach.

Rose petals were strewn about, candles the cottage's current main source of light.

Oh, boy.

"You don't like pink?" he asked.

"Contrary to the movie title, I don't look pretty in pink, but it's fine. You going to carry me over the threshold or what?"

"We're not married," he reminded her, following her when she strode on inside.

As was his habit, he checked for possible exits, as well as the best places to hide his stash of weapons, cash and passports he still had hidden under floorboards and behind pictures in his old cottage down the beach.

Ginger took off the Celtic ring, setting it on a nearby dresser.

On the way over from the party they'd decided to run with their fake engagement and enjoy the added perks of winning the bigger cottage—which wasn't bigger, of course, just...more intimate. As an engaged couple, they would also continue to be able to get into the parties and possibly make better deals as a result.

Plus Ginger was darn cute and lightened his mood when

she was around, and he was still hoping she might be the answer to his visa issue.

But suddenly it all felt a bit uncomfortable.

"I'll take the couch," he said, kicking back in its overstuffed cushions. He pulled a wrapped chocolate from the box placed on the coffee table. He unwrapped it and popped it in his mouth, then tossed one to Ginger, who was standing near the bed in the other room—a fancy affair partially hidden behind netting draped from the ceiling.

"They packed my suitcase." She didn't catch the treat and it hit the floor at her feet.

"Yeah, weird feeling." He didn't like the idea of anyone touching his things, even if he hadn't left anything sensitive out in the open.

He tossed another chocolate her way.

"This is pretty insane," she said, catching it absently.

"Agreed."

"You stargaze?" She pointed to the telescope that had been brought to the cottage. He typically spent more time spying with it, but occasionally aimed it at the sky.

"Hobbiest." He pulled the bottle of champagne from its ice bucket.

"You take your telescope on vacation? No." She shook her head. "You work in town, but stay at the resort?"

"Monthly rental." Close to his target, Vito. A target that might pursue Ginger to get to him if he wasn't very careful. "Champagne?"

She pursed her lips, then nodded, snagging one of the crystal flutes from the table. She looked uncertain, nervous. He didn't blame her, really. At the party everyone had been excited for them. Add in the attention and fun of it all, and it had been easy to get caught up in it. Now she was sharing a cottage with a stranger. A deadly male stranger, in fact. Although he was honorable. That should count for something.

Still, if he'd had a sister, he wouldn't want her in Ginger's position.

"Truth or dare?" Logan suggested.

"Dare?" She choked on a laugh. "Do you really think *that's* a good idea?"

"Are you chicken?" he asked, slowly leaning forward.

She blushed. He needed her to trust him, help him. And right now, the way she was acting, he'd be surprised to find her still at his side come morning.

"I'll go first," he suggested.

"No, I will." She paused to think, jumping when he popped open the champagne, sending the cork ricocheting off the ceiling.

He laughed. "Oops." He poured her a glass, handing it over before she sank into the armchair across from him.

"Truth," she said. "Are you always this carefree? Not caring about the rules and being honest?"

She was regretting their lies.

"That's more than one question."

"Is this who you really are?"

"Nope." He couldn't meet her eyes.

"How many women have you kissed?"

"My turn." Wow. She was really digging into the good stuff. He needed to turn this around. Get her to trust him, play along without thinking so much or trying to reveal his tender underbelly. Assuming he still had one.

He needed something...lighthearted that would bring out

the good time and allow her get carried away with him and the craziness of their situation. Anything but think about the fact that they were two dishonest people. "I dare you to go outside and yodel from the front steps."

She sighed as if it was the most immature thing she'd ever heard, but stood up, straightened her green dress and shimmied to the front door. She hauled it open, marched to the top of the steps and, with her hands on her hips, bellowed, "Yodel-lay-he-hoo!" She turned to give him a sassy look.

He chuckled and shook his head from where he'd leaned past the couch to watch her.

Someone replied with yodel from far off down the beach.

Laughing, Ginger came back inside, closing the door behind her. She collapsed into her armchair with an endearing case of the giggles. Her dress rode up, revealing extra flesh above her knee. She had gorgeous legs. Strong, smooth.

"I wouldn't have predicted you'd do that," he admitted.

"That's because you don't know me."

"I bet your still sleep with a teddy bear names Roses."

She smiled over the rim of her glass and he couldn't tell if she was amused by how off base he was or if he'd hit close to the truth.

"Your worst fear?" she asked.

"Why the heavy stuff?"

"Why are you such a baby?" she retorted.

"I'm not a baby." He didn't think anyone had ever called him that. He wanted to pull out his rap sheet and prove just how tough he truly was.

Obviously, that would blow his cover, though. And

probably send her flying over the sand dunes faster than a souped up dune buggy.

"Then tell me your worst fear."

"Fine." He pushed back into the sofa, trying for casual. "That I'm going to hurt the people I'm trying to help."

And...he probably shouldn't have said that.

She gave him a soft look, and before she could go squishy on him or figure out why a wholesaler was worried about hurting people, he asked, "What's *your* worst fear?"

"Being lied to. And how are you going to hurt anyone in your line of work?"

Of course. There was that sharp awareness he'd seen earlier. He shouldn't be surprised it was popping up.

"How is being lied to a worst fear?" People lied all the time. For example, how many times had they done so that night? Then again, he was a spy. That was what he did for a living—lied. But her? Nobody would get hurt if the truth came out about their charade. They might have to forfeit a few prizes, and pay for the upgrade, probably, but otherwise...not exactly worst-fear material.

"Obviously you haven't had someone close to you lie when and where it counts."

Ouch.

And an entirely wrong assumption.

"Did he cheat?" Logan asked.

"Truth. Do you snore?"

"Aren't I supposed to choose whether it's truth or a dare? We're playing wrong."

But he knew one more thing about her. Her ex had cheated. Lied.

As a result, she had baggage and was vulnerable. Somehow

that just made her more intriguing to him, made him want to be more careful with her.

Still, Logan wanted to find the man and sock him one for hurting her. Not that he himself planned to do any better. He was currently waltzing into her life with lies and deception, encouraging her to take part in his dangerous charade. Then he would suddenly spin around and vanish, leaving her bubbly self a crying mess.

He was already worse than the last guy.

However, Ginger wasn't the only smart one in the room. Logan could use his wiles to protect her from getting hurt, and he'd become nothing but a fond memory during a time when she'd let herself be free and broke a few rules. She would never know the truth or how he'd used her.

That was a promise he could keep.

But first he had to convince her to walk down the aisle with him. And that...that might be more difficult than shooting the button out of a security system from fifty yards. Except he could do that.

"I bet you snore as loud as a fighter jet," she teased, when he didn't reply.

"I think that'll be something you'll have to find out on your own."

"Maybe I don't plan on sleeping."

"Maybe I don't, either."

"Are you married or have you been?"

"You didn't wait for your turn."

"You're sure into the rules, for someone who just broke about eighty of them an hour ago. What's your biggest secret, Logan Stone?"

"If I tell you, I'd have to kill you."

She shivered and he worried he'd accidentally said it like he meant it. He went for a quick cover. "Truth—are you going to kiss me again tonight?"

"You kissed me, buster."

"And you liked it."

"So did you."

He smiled, enjoying the way she stood up to him, dished it back and didn't take any of his guff. She was a challenge. A good one. And because of that he had a pretty good feeling that Ginger was not only going to distract him in all the ways that were most enjoyable, but probably change his life. He just hoped she'd also help him complete this mission.

GINGER TENSED. SOMETHING HAD WOKEN her and she squeaked as she spied a large form move across the unfamiliar bedroom. Where was she? Why was there a mess of suffocating curtains around her bed?

"It's just me, Logan," said a deep voice.

Oh, it was her dream man, Logan Stone. Her roommate and fake fiancé for the next few days. How had she ended up in such a pickle?

Right. Her new fetish for lying and her insatiable greed for prizes. What had been in that wine?

Logan wasn't a bad prize, though. In the moonlight she could see him moving around the room as he got himself a glass of water. He was in jeans and a T-shirt. Not pajamas.

"Can't sleep?" she asked, stretching out in the comfy bed. She checked the time. It was three in the morning. Hardly time to give up on sleep.

"I went for a walk. The moon's beautiful."

"At this time of night?" She propped herself up on an elbow. "Well, I guess you don't have to worry about being attacked when you're the size of a cottage."

He let out a soft chuckle.

"So what does being a diamond wholesaler actually mean?"

They'd played a teasing round of truth or dare, where they'd basically just parried back and forth, skirting their issues. He was a private person and she could understand him not wanting to open up to someone he'd just met. Even if he was pretending to be close enough to her that he wanted to marry her.

"Basically, I'm a glorified salesman."

"I own a bridal shop, which sounds amazing, but at the end of the day, basically I'm a glorified salesperson, too. But didn't you say you're from a ranch in Australia? Why would you come to sell diamonds here in America?"

"Life led me here."

Life. It had a way of doing that, didn't it? Sending you in directions you could never have expected. When her parents had broken up, she'd been a teen and had started working in her grandmother's store as a distraction. She'd found her solace there. The idea that some marriages would and could last, that love could light up a person's whole world. And seeing the brides so happy and alive had given her hope that real love and fidelity existed.

Ginger had thought she'd found it with her high school boyfriend. But then Kurt hadn't gone to college with her. She'd been accepted into a state university across the country and he'd settled for a local college, leaving her.

Just like Logan would leave. Same ending. Different story. Very different.

The two were silent for some time, Logan returning to the couch to lay on his back, arm behind his head. Ginger snuggled onto her side, watching him through a break in the bed's curtains.

She thought of her hometown of Blueberry Springs. It was a quiet mountain community, full of miners, ranchers, businessmen and everyone in between. It was a busybody kind of place, where everyone knew everyone and was there in a heartbeat when there was a need. Towns like that got under one's skin, became a big part of who you were. She couldn't imagine moving away for any length of time, let alone working on a whole different continent.

"Do you miss the ranch?"

Logan paused, then gave a sigh. "Sometimes."

"What do you miss most?"

"The space to think," he replied immediately.

"Yeah?"

"Yeah."

She looked over at him. He barely fit on that piece of furniture and she felt bad for taking the bed.

"We should trade spots. You're too long for the couch."

"What kind of man would I be if I took the bed?"

"One who could actually get some sleep."

They were quiet for another long moment. Silence with him didn't feel awkward. In a crazy way, it felt like bonding.

Totally crazy.

"You know I went to college not far from here," she offered.

"What did you take?"

"Business."

"And now you're in business." He shifted on the couch. No doubt trying to get comfortable.

"Did you go to school?"

"I was in the army for a bit. They taught me a few things."

"Like how to kiss forty women?"

"Forty?"

"Nine hundred?" She propped herself up on an elbow. "How many?" She was dying to know. A man who kissed like he did...he had to have practiced a *lot*, and a part of her wanted to know how many others she was being measured against. Self-defeating for certain. But fighting her curiosity had never been one of her strengths.

"Not that many."

"Five hundred?"

"You think I'm a horny old bull from the station, don't you?"

"Station?"

"The Aussie equivalent of a ranch."

"Oh."

As he shifted on the couch again, trying to get comfortable, she threw back the covers, determined to make the switch. She went and stood over him. "Come on. Take the bed." He didn't budge. "Mo-o-ove!"

He crossed his arms across his sculpted chest. "Did you just moo at me?"

"You randy old bull, get going. Mush."

"Mush?" He laughed. The skin around his eyes crinkled when he did, lightening up his expression, which was usually so serious.

"Git. Git along, little doggies."

He let out a loud guffaw. She pulled at his arm, barely budging him.

"If you can move me, we'll trade. And the number is well less than a hundred—not including cheek kisses."

She pulled harder. No luck. She pretended to give up, then dived for his sides, ticking him. His body curled up protectively, tipping her on top of him as she continued her attack. He squirmed, his laugh big and loud.

"Stop," he cried, helpless with laughter.

"Did I move you enough to win?"

"No. Never. I'm not ticklish."

She continued her onslaught until he was breathless with laughter. Mr. Tough Guy was *so* unbelievably ticklish.

He tried to attack back, but she clamped her elbows at her sides. The two of them tumbled off the couch, his hands going to either side of her so he didn't crush her as he landed. She became aware of the heat that radiated from him, and his laughter quieted.

She wanted to give in to the pull that would have them kissing in seconds.

He planned to go home to his ranch. He wasn't going to stay here.

Nothing serious would come from them succumbing to their desire and sharing one little steamy kiss on the floor of their honeymoon cottage. She wouldn't get involved, just have a little fun without the happily-ever-after expectation that always seemed to rear up in her.

Perfect, in other words.

"Logan?" she said softly.

"Hmm?" He was watching her with those steady gray eyes of his, taking in every inch of her, making her feel grounded.

LOGAN HAD ENJOYED A FRESH, delivered breakfast on the small veranda of the honeymoon cottage he was sharing with Ginger. Then he'd kissed her goodbye, just the way he'd kissed her last night. Slow, deep and completely consuming.

Every time he kissed her he had to reorient himself afterward.

There was just something about that woman.

Even without an audience, he was finding himself kissing her when there was no need to put on a show. And he'd found her hand slipping into his when it was only the two of them sharing a meal in private.

Somehow, his least likely option for a visa had become his best.

And yet what he felt around Ginger was more than just a spy game. It was the start of something. A short-term love affair? A fling? A snapshot of what it could be like if he left his world behind and rejoined humanity?

He needed her close, needed her to trust him. And that was happening. He really shouldn't think any further than that, even though he knew he had to. Lives depended upon it.

From the veranda, he watched her hips sway in that mesmerizing way as she walked barefoot down the sandy shore toward her morning workshop, enjoying the day, her sandals hooked in her fingers. That's what he liked most about her, he decided. She was genuine. Ready to relish every bit of life that came her way. She took nothing for granted, expected nothing in return.

He waited until she was out of sight, shortly after which their personal butler reappeared in his golf cart to clear away their dishes. Over breakfast, Ginger had managed to convince the man to phone a woman she'd met a few days prior and ask her to join him at the festival going on in town. Neither had someone to go with, so Ginger had taken matters into her own hands, as Logan was starting to realize was the norm for her. She was a sweet little matchmaker, something he found charming.

He tipped the butler, wishing him luck with his festival date. Then, when the coast was clear, Logan double-checked where he'd hidden most of his retrieved weapons and gadgets before Ginger had awakened last night, and, satisfied that all was well, headed down the beach in the opposite direction from his fake fiancée.

He walked for miles, avoiding Seaside Boulevard, which served the cottages. He dropped into his office, which was part of his cover, and tipped his imaginary hat to the police officer, Paul, who was stationed outside, watching for any form of visa abuse. Logan took some razzing from his two employees, who thought their jobs were legit, and continued on, stopping in the shadows here and there to ensure that no one, not even Paul, was following him. Several blocks later, he buzzed to be let into a sprawling old mansion that had been refurbished into an assisted living facility, the Indigo Bay Manor. He was feeling optimistic that he could count on Ginger to come through for him with a marriage by Wednesday, even though it was already Monday. But in case it fell apart and he found himself being deported, he needed to ensure that Annabelle Babkins had a heads-up.

He'd avoided telling her he might have to leave, knowing that sometimes the best option came in a moment of true desperation. But with two days left, it was time to tell her, so he didn't suddenly vanish and leave her alarmed.

"Hi, Logan." One of the pretty nurses, Gabby, met him at the locked doors, letting him in. "Annabelle's just getting ready to go to work."

Nobody but the director knew he was Annabelle's guardian; the rest of the staff simply thought he was a good man who volunteered to walk her to work two times a week, as well as play cards with the group on Fridays. Hiding her in plain sight. That's what he was doing for his late pal Rogue Babkins. Logan had had to move Annabelle from Florida last year, unable to care for her that far away. It was a big risk, settling her close to where he was working, but she didn't know enough to blow his cover, and what else could he do? Abandon her after her father's death?

Gabby gave him a spontaneous squeeze, filling the air around him with a lemon scent. "You're so good with her."

"As are you."

"How do I snag a man like you? You volunteer here, at the animal shelter, and tutor kids. You're gold."

"And engaged," he said with a smile.

"Tell your lucky duck that I hate her already." The nurse gave him a wink and went back to her desk.

Logan walked down a narrow hall on the main floor, where the more independent residents had their private rooms. He felt a cloud shift over his mood. How was he going to move Annabelle from here? She was thriving, starting to open up and live again. She was forging ahead, discovering independence on a whole new level, with her job setting tables at a local restaurant two days a week.

Moving her to Australia wasn't a good option. And neither was leaving her behind.

He absently knocked on her door as Lucille Sanderson came around the corner. She was a well-known busybody in her seventies, and had nothing better to do than ride him about his single status. If there was anyone who could unearth and expose an undercover agent, it was a woman like Lucille.

"Come in!" called Annabelle.

"Oh, Logan!" chirped Lucille, as he reached for the doorknob. "Logan!" She waved, her high heels taking her as fast as she could go, her still-blond hair tucked into a loose bun. "I've set you up on a blind date with my great-niece Maggie from Georgia this Friday. She's such a doll. You'll love her."

"Too late. I got engaged, Lucille."

"No," she breathed, her eyes round as she came to a halt. He got the distinct feeling she didn't believe him.

"Crazy, I know!" He gave her a big smile and opened the door, slipping inside before Annabelle could overhear the news of his newly acquired and fake relationship status. He casually held a hand against the door in case Lucille tried to shoulder her way in. He figured she was too polite, but wasn't entirely confident that would stop her this time.

Annabelle had been sitting in front of her vanity, carefully combing her fine blond hair. At eighteen she was legally an adult, but due to Down syndrome she wasn't able to be as independent as the average young woman and was still learning a lot of life skills most teens took for granted.

"You look gorgeous as usual," Logan said. She beamed and set down her comb, carefully lining it up with her brush before jumping up, giving him an enthusiastic, warm hug. "I'm here to walk you to work."

He handed her the knit purse he'd bought her for her birthday down at the local market. It was pink with a striped background behind a solitary flower—stripes being her favorite "shape." Today she was wearing her red-white-and-blue-striped shirt. One of many. In fact, pretty much everything in her room had stripes, from her brush to her bedspread. It was dizzying and disorienting, but she loved it.

"Say something Aussie," she demanded.

"All right, you pretty little sheila, let's get a move on and have a good day, mate."

She cracked up and they began walking down the hall. He signed her out of the manor even though she could sign herself out if she talked to one of the staff first.

As they walked along the boardwalk toward the restaurant, he wondered how he was going to prep her for his absence. He'd already arranged for the manor to act as her guardian in his absence, but he didn't know how the next few months were going to pan out. If he took another mission, he could go dark for some time, which would worry her, and she deserved more than that. She needed someone present, someone she could rely on.

"Ever think of moving somewhere different?" he asked. A half block up from the boardwalk he could see Officer Paul patrolling a pay-by-the-hour parking lot, looking for expired tags. Logan quickly ushered Annabelle farther down the boardwalk, out of the man's sight so as to avoid any discussion with him about his soon-to-expire visa.

"I moved here." Annabelle gave him a stubborn look.

"And it's awesome."

"I want to ski."

"Ski?" he asked in surprise.

"I saw it on TV. I want to learn and I need mountains."

"Downhill?"

She nodded vigorously. "I like mountains. Snow. Snowflakes."

"You've never seen winter."

"I like it."

He could envision her enjoying the wonders of winter. That would be a fun sight to watch. The pure joy.

"How do you feel about Australia? They have skiing. We could move there." He could move her in the dead of the night when he had to leave. He wouldn't need a visa for her right away, and months ago he'd ordered her a passport as a precaution. He could tell her it was a trip, then pull the she's-my-dependent card with officials to get her papers to stay in Oz. She wouldn't be happy, but they'd be together.

If he didn't take another mission.

Annabelle was silent for a moment, thinking, leaving nothing but the sounds of their feet hitting the boardwalk and the gulls crying overhead.

He glanced in the direction of the marina where Vito kept his yacht. He'd need to get on board before Thursday and bug it. Get Ginger to marry him before then.

"Wallabies?" Annabelle asked, trying to imitate his accent.

"Wallabies. Koalas. Kangaroos."

She stared at him for a moment, then burst into tears.

Logan stopped, uncertain what had triggered the waterworks. "You all right, mate?"

She cried harder.

He must have a kangaroo loose in his top paddock, or as Americans said "a screw loose" telling her out here in public. He glanced around for Lucille, knowing she'd immediately see right through his "mere volunteer" status and blow everything wide-open. He'd wanted to avoid anyone in the center, including the visiting Lucille, figuring out their connection—the less they knew, the better protected Annabelle was. But right now? Anyone tailing him might twig that something was up and that he wasn't just a volunteer escorting her to work.

"What's wrong?" He led her to a bench and sat her down.

"I like my flag."

"Your flag?"

"Australia doesn't have stripes."

"Well, they sort of do—the union jack."

"Those aren't stripes!"

"But we have stars. And the same colors."

"I want stripes."

Crikey. That could be a deal breaker for someone like Annabelle. As odd as it might seem to outsiders, it made perfect sense to Logan. She liked stripes and they made her feel happy, secure.

"You're very patriotic, aren't you, AnnaBee?" The nickname didn't make her smile, either. "You could put up an American flag in Australia, you know. Lots of people do it."

Not lots, but a few expats.

"Are you leaving?" She stood up again, fists balled.

To her, leaving and death had become twisted into one thing, and he had to tread carefully. "I'm not leaving. We could go together."

"No!"

"Like when we came here," he explained quickly. "It would be just like that."

"Dad died! He was leaving. He's dead. I don't want to be dead."

"Nobody's going to die. Nothing's for sure, okay?"

She cried harder, as if she knew he was lying, and he felt like a heel for dealing her such a high level of unexpected heartbreak. He had to find a way to stay beyond Wednesday, beyond the next mission. He needed Ginger for more than just capturing Vito.

GINGER SOAKED UP THE SUN AS she headed toward the boardwalk for a little mind-emptying stroll between sessions. She was full of ideas and knew that even though the trip was close to breaking her financially, she was going to return to Blueberry Springs energized and full of lucrative new plans. Her store was popular, thanks to the hard work that Wanda had put into it, and brides traveled for miles to shop there. Ginger had plans on how to expand upon that, reduce her overhead costs and really knock the business to the next level.

She could do it, and once she did she'd finally feel like she had something—a purpose. That she was more than just a boring, small-town woman with a cute store.

Letting her mind drift, Ginger passed the Tiki Hut bar nestled in the sand. Kelso was chatting with Vicky, who was behind the polished driftwood counter, and Ginger gave him a subtle thumbs-up, which he returned with a smile while pointing her out. Vicky turned, all smiles.

A match! Nice.

Up on the boardwalk, Ginger found herself wandering in

the direction of the coffee shop that had provided her and Logan with their breakfast, and that Zoe from the cottages' guest services had mentioned. She could afford a fancy coffee now that her stay was covered by the honeymoon win, and feeling buoyed by how much fun she'd had letting loose with Logan—dreamy, impossibly good kisser Logan Stone—she sighed and just about tripped off the curb while crossing the street. An older man caught her with a "Whoopsy daisy there, little lass."

Ginger thanked him while laughing at herself. Talk about having her head in the clouds!

Before long she found Sweet Caroline's, with the signature blue awning. As she opened the door she was assaulted by an influx of amazing smells that reminded her of Mandy's little cafe back home. Cinnamon, sugar, butter. Coffee.

"I love the smell of this place," said a man coming in behind her as he caught her inhaling deeply, eyes closed.

"Me, too," Ginger replied, opening her eyes.

"My last girlfriend claimed I made her fat because I'd come home smelling like this place."

"For real?" Ginger glanced at the man. He seemed serious.

"For real."

"Hmm. Are you still single? I know a woman down at the cottages who happens to love this place and all its fattening flavors and aromas."

"Give her my number," the man said with a laugh.

Ginger held out her hand with a smile. "I will. My name's Ginger. Hers is Zoe, and she has a particular thing for the cinnamon buns."

The man blinked in surprise. Then, as if unable to think of a reason not to, wrote his number on a napkin and handed it to her. "Why not? I love the cinnamon buns, too. As well as Caroline's award-winning pie. And her cobbler. I'm Ash—short for Ashton. I obviously work out a lot so I can eat here whenever I want." He gave a warm smile, as rich as the coffee Ginger planned on ordering.

"Well, Ash, expect Zoe's call," Ginger said, waving the napkin and knowing the two would make an adorable couple.

And, hey, if you couldn't find a match for yourself, why not meddle in the love lives of others?

She stepped toward the counter, where a woman in her fifties was talking to a customer a mile a minute about someone named Lucille being madder than a wet hen because the man she'd set her great-niece up with on a date was now supposedly engaged.

"Not that I blame him," the woman behind the counter said. Her name tag read Caroline and her apparent knowledge of all gossip reminded Ginger of Mary Alice from back home. "Once Lucille gets an idea in her head...well, look out!"

"Tell me about it," the customer grumbled. "Add her to the Stuck-up Club and ho boy."

"Now, now," said the woman behind the counter as she handed over her order. "The Ashland Belle Society isn't all bad. They do a lot of good things for the town."

"I know, I know. But they can be a bit high-and-mighty at times."

"Can't we all?"

The two smiled in agreement.

"Now dear," Caroline said, looking to Ginger, "what can I get for you?"

"A mocha please. Double shot of chocolate if you can."

"No, honey, you want my sweet tea on a day like today." Caroline began pouring Ginger a clear plastic cup of cold tea.

Ginger looked at it doubtfully. "I like my tea hot."

"You're not from around here, are you?"

"No, ma'am."

"The north?"

"And west."

"Well, down South we drink it cold." She handed her the tea at no charge and called out as Ginger left, "Don't be a stranger, you hear?"

Ginger nodded and waved, with another thanks.

Wow. She was definitely like Mary Alice.

But free sweet tea? She could handle that. She took a sip and stopped in surprise. She backtracked to the cafe and hollered inside, "It's good!"

"Of course it's good," the woman huffed. "I made it myself!"

Ginger laughed and returned to the boardwalk, feeling as though her life was finally making a nice turn. One where she'd start getting what she'd set her sights on so long ago. One where luck was on her side. One with fun.

Lots more fun.

And speaking of fun, she saw a familiar, hunky man up ahead. Logan. Her heart lifted and her pace increased before she caught herself. Logan had a real life in Indigo Bay that didn't include her and their temporary charade. And apparently his real life included a crying, flailing woman.

Uh-oh.

Ginger began slowly backing away, mesmerized with how

lost Mr. Take Charge Logan appeared in the situation. He was standing there, body slack, hands loose at his sides.

He turned, thrusting his hands through the hair at his temples, looking around as though aware he was being watched. His dejected body language dropped as he spotted her down the boardwalk and he perked up before quickly catching himself and acting cavalier.

Ginger smiled, knowing that Logan liked her.

She wanted to say hi, but the woman he was with didn't exactly need an audience.

Was Logan breaking up with whomever it was? That idea made Ginger feel sick to her stomach.

"Die!" the woman yelled.

Oh, wow. Okay. Very bad breakup. Ginger began backpedaling faster.

Was it because of her they were breaking up? That hardly seemed to fit the picture of last night and this morning. Then again, she'd proved to be a good target for liars.

The woman was still crying and shouting, her voice thick, her tears out of control. Ginger found herself moving closer, wishing to comfort her, explain that Logan was...the best kisser on planet earth and that they'd shared a honeymoon cottage last night and had kind of won an elopement wedding package?

Maybe not. But as she drew near she discovered the crying woman was actually a teenager who, judging from the set of her eyes, had Down syndrome.

"You guys okay?" Ginger asked gently, shifting herself onto the bench where the young woman was sitting.

"Nope. Not okay." Logan's lips twisted.

"Can I help?"

"He's leaving me!" the girl cried, finger raised at Logan. "Dead!"

"She's my...I'm her guardian," Logan explained quietly.

Okay, Ginger hadn't seen that one coming.

"She lives a few blocks from here and I'm walking her to work and we started talking and...well..."

"But you live in Australia," Ginger said stupidly. How could he be a guardian of someone here?

"Yes."

"And you're leaving in two days."

The girl wailed louder, causing more people to look their way. "Dead!"

Ginger put a hand gently on her shoulder, surprised when she turned toward her and fell into her arms, sobbing in anguish. Ginger held her close and patted her back comfortingly before glancing up at Logan. "Are you, um...?"

"Dying? No." He rubbed a knuckle against his forehead and sighed. "Moving? Well, you know the story."

The visa issue. She squeezed the girl tighter. Now the pieces were starting to fall into place.

"You have a ranch," Ginger said. "You two could—"

"There's nothing," Logan said grimly.

"But..." He'd said there was a ranch. Was he a liar? Or had she misunderstood him? "You said you miss it."

"I do. I sold it when my wife left—went to the city," he quickly amended. He turned to the girl, crouching to make eye contact. "There are mountains in Australia, Annabelle."

"No stripes!" she yelled back, throwing herself out of Ginger's embrace.

"I can paint your room in stripes. Any color."

The girl's tears were still falling, but she was watching him from the corner of her eye now. Logan perched on the boardwalk in front of the bench. "I'm not leaving you. And if you want stripes everywhere, that's what I'll get you. You and I are sticking together."

Ginger felt her heart melt. This was a man who was not leaving for anything, and that made her want to help him in any way she could.

CHAPTER 3

Logan awoke, immediately on high alert. He was on his feet, his back pressed against the wall before he'd even sorted out where he was.

Indigo Bay. Honeymoon cottage.

He'd broken Annabelle's heart, then come back to crash, feeling like the world's biggest jerk.

"Logan?"

It was Ginger.

His adrenaline started to wash away and he relaxed. He stepped around the corner to greet her at the cottage's entry. "Hey."

"Were you sleeping?" In the crook of her left arm was a bundle of brochures and notes from her day's workshops.

He rubbed his eyes. "No."

"Liar." She planted her free hand in the middle of his chest, giving him a push. "What did I say about liars?"

"You hate them." He caught her hand and took in her capris and T-shirt. "Funny you say that, since your pants are currently on fire there, my little fibber. You should take them off."

"Ha." She dropped her bundle onto the bed and frowned.

"Goldilocks was sleeping on my bed." She gave him a sly smile. "Told you you should have it. It's comfy, isn't it?"

"Sorry, I was tired. I'll keep the couch tonight."

"Logan." She gently placed a hand on his arm. "Take the bed. It's okay." She was studying him in a way that told him she was thinking about Annabelle's meltdown on the boardwalk.

In the end, Ginger had managed to calm her enough that she could be walked to work. Ginger had been awesome, chatting about this and that until the girl was her usual cheery self again. Meanwhile, Logan had trailed behind like a rejected dog so as not to upset her any further. Ginger was good with Annabelle and he'd found himself wondering if there was a way she could help out if he got himself deported. He didn't think so, though, since she was from the other side of the country and couldn't exactly pop in to put her back together again if she was having a tough day. Couldn't drop by to celebrate the kid's birthday or other holidays, either.

If he left, she'd be alone.

If he got deported on Wednesday, months of work on this case would go up in smoke.

Every way he moved on this case, with staying close to Annabelle, there was a roadblock. And even worse, he'd slept the entire afternoon away, meaning he hadn't had a chance to take care of bugging Vito's yacht or discovering who else would be at Thursday's meeting so he'd know what he was walking into, stepping aboard.

"Annabelle is okay?" Ginger asked.

"Yeah. Can you swim?"

"Yes. Why? You want to go swimming?"

He shook his head. If things went south on the yacht he

could swim ashore, even if they were miles out. But Ginger...he'd have to make sure he threw a floatation device in the water for her, or find a way to keep her on land.

What was he thinking?

Things wouldn't go south. It would all be okay. He'd taken down men worse than Vito, and the yacht trip wouldn't be the actual arrest, anyway. It would be the lynchpin in the case when it came to evidence, because it wasn't like Vito was suddenly going to unearth his thirty-three-million-dollar stash of conflict diamonds there on the boat.

Logan needed at least another week. Maybe two.

But before any of that he had to convince Ginger to marry him.

"Logan?" She was looking at him like his mind had been elsewhere, which it had. "Annabelle seemed really upset."

He nodded. "She has issues with people leaving."

He wished Ginger hadn't seen them, wished she didn't know something real and vulnerable about him. Not because he didn't trust her or want her to know—it actually felt nice having someone to talk to. But anything real could be used against him in his line of work. He'd been careful for an entire year, then in walks a gorgeous sheila and he was close to blowing it all. Now there was a link from him to Ginger. Ginger to Annabelle. From Annabelle to him. From her to her father, Rogue. From Rogue to Logan.

Not good. Trails were bad. Very bad. There had been one before, but it had been a vague trail, one he'd tracked over so badly that it was difficult for anyone to follow. And if they did manage to get a lead, he'd see it in enough time that he'd be able to hide Annabelle. The situation had been as close to safe as he could get without abandoning the kid. But now? It was like a spider web, with each trail leading into the middle, where he sat like a spider, hoping not to be seen by prey larger than himself.

"What about her family?"

"I'm it."

The memory of Rogue's last words, begging him to take care of Annabelle flitted, through his mind.

"Just you?"

"There's nobody else," he whispered.

"And there's no way to get your visa extended or to keep you here somehow?"

"Not legally."

Ginger didn't press any further, simply wrapped her arms around him, her face creased with an uncharacteristic frown. She was so small, her hands barely reached past each other behind his back as she flattened them against his spine. And yet he felt engulfed. Engulfed by someone who cared, who wanted him to feel better. He hadn't known someone like that in a long time, other than his AnnaBee.

Logan allowed himself the moment, allowed himself to borrow strength from someone else for once.

He was so darn exhausted.

Ginger laid her head against his chest and he wondered if his heart, which had been broken by life so many times, sounded normal to her ear. He gently rested his cheek on top of her head, feeling his mind drifting without its usual turmoil of thoughts.

Home.

He felt peace, and caught himself falling, his body jerking upright again.

"Did you just fall asleep?" Ginger asked, her voice tinged with humor.

"I think I did," he said in wonder. That was a first. At times during missions he'd felt like falling asleep on his feet, but had never been able to let his guard down enough to actually accomplish the feat.

Doing so now meant Ginger was bad news.

Or good news.

He still wasn't sure which.

GINGER GLANCED UP AT LOGAN, who was walking alongside her, the waves lapping at their feet as they headed toward the evening's event for engaged couples. Annabelle had been so overwrought, so full of heartbreak that afternoon. The poor gal had nobody but Logan, and he was leaving in less than forty-eight hours.

Just thinking about it made Ginger's chest tighten with a sense of loss. She knew what it was like to have the father figure in your life suddenly leave. But she at least still had her mother, Wanda, and the store that fulfilled her fantasies of a happily ever after.

Annabelle had nobody.

Just a man who wanted to stay, but couldn't. And the helpless look in his eyes while he'd stood there on the boardwalk had nearly done Ginger in. His willingness to help a friend's daughter made him special, and gave him a certain permanence that the other foreign men she'd dated had lacked, something real that couldn't be faked. Logan was doing everything in his power *not* to leave.

And to be torn like that. Having to go home because your visa was expiring, but having responsibility here...how could he have let it get this close to disaster? She knew he was smart and wouldn't have left this to chance, but still. Everything had to be conspiring against him. She wished there was a way to help him stay in South Carolina.

"Do you want to go back to Australia?" she asked, hooking her hand in his.

"I have a lot keeping me here right now."

"Annabelle."

He nodded. "She's adamant she doesn't want to leave with me, and that was my backup plan if my visa didn't come through—which it hasn't."

"And your job is keeping you here, too?"

He looked at her in surprise.

"Diamond wholesaler," she reminded him. "Very sought after. Once you land that you don't just give it up on a whim."

He laughed. "True."

She smiled as Kelso and Vicky came along the sand together, heading in the opposite direction. Ginger gave them a wink and they lifted their linked hands.

"Thanks, Ginger," Kelso said as they passed.

"Anytime."

"What was that about?" Logan asked.

She shrugged. "Just helping two people find the right person."

He turned so he was walking backward, facing her. "You're a matchmaker, aren't you?"

"Sometimes." It was an easy problem to fix, unlike most of life.

"My sweet little matchmaker." Logan gave her hand a

gentle squeeze, infusing her with warmth. His grip, like him, was gentle, but also strong and sure. With Logan at her side their whole charade somehow felt as solid as the ring on her finger, like the man himself, and she found herself wishing for more time to explore the connection.

"You said Annabelle is your dependent? You're legally responsible for her?"

"I am. She's eighteen now, though."

"What does that mean?"

"Basically, I either leave her behind or I take her with me, but she gets a say."

"And she says no?"

He sighed and rubbed her brow. "Yeah. And I don't blame her. It's only been a year since I moved her here after her father died. It was a big adjustment, and now I'm asking her to make another one. She likes it here, loves her job. She's starting to thrive and we'd be taking a huge step back, moving her across the world. But if I leave, she's abandoned all over again and would become a part of the system without an outside advocate."

"Is her mom gone, too?"

"She's not interested."

"So it's you."

He exhaled unsteadily, and she could tell just how much this was pulling on him even though he was trying to hide it.

"So why don't you marry an American and stay?"

"And who would I marry?" They'd stopped walking and Logan stooped to pick up a seashell, rubbing his thumb along its smooth contours, avoiding her eyes.

"Me."

There. She'd said it.

Logan didn't reply, just tipped his head, peering at her through his lashes.

Oh, so serious.

"The resort will take care of everything with their nutso but well-timed elopement package, then you can stay." She gave a light shrug. It wasn't love, but it was a good reason to get married. Plus it would give her time to reevaluate her life, get involved in her new work projects, let her heart heal without thinking she should get back into the dating game. There were two good reasons right there: Annabelle and Ginger's heart. Plus there was that whole forbidden whisper she kept shoving to the back of her mind. The one that kept suggesting maybe a marriage of convenience was just what she needed, and would turn out like her grandmother's forty-seven wonderful years of happily ever after.

Logan remained silent and Ginger braced herself. "Did I put too much out there? Too desperate?" she joked. Inside, she was dying. He wasn't saying a thing. Not even freaking out. Was it because he'd been married before and couldn't stand the idea of jumping into matrimony again? Especially with a stranger?

Panic was setting in fast, sinking her hopes and pride like they were tied to a stone.

"I'm not in love, or some desperate crazy person, you know," she said quickly. "I just see it as a good solution."

"A fake marriage," he said quietly. He looked doubtful, not relieved like she'd hoped.

She dropped her hands on her hips, putting her best glare to use. "Yes. It doesn't have to be a crime, you know." She could see what he was thinking—that he was likely worrying about the legalities. "We're the good guys, two friends who

like each other and want to help each other and who might
go on dates sometimes, right?"

"Dates?" The corner of his lips turned up.

"Why not? You're cute. I'm cute. That can't be illegal.
Besides, the government does worse than a marriage of
convenience all the time—why would they even bother with
us? We're doing a good thing here, relieving the burden on
the system, with you helping Annabelle and encouraging her
to be gainfully employed and a contributing member of
society. If you leave, I'm certain it will cost the country more
than if you stay—and staying brings in income tax, too.
Right? The country comes out ahead and they can't prove
whether we love each other or not.

"And anyway, the government is more worried about
overtaxing my business because it's a nonessential service,
even though my store brings people into town who then shop
in other stores and eat in restaurants. You'd think the mayor
would understand that he's killing us all with taxation. And
don't even get me started on health care, child support and
federal—"

"You have a child?"

Whoops. She'd kind of gone on a rant by accident.

She shook off her outrage and indignation.

"No kids, but I was one." Her father had totally shirked
helping her mom financially, and the government hadn't been
especially helpful with rounding up child support.

Not that she now wanted to stick it to the government as
some form of delayed retribution, but in the grand scheme of
things her marrying a man she'd developed a crush on so he
could stay with a girl who needed him...well, that hardly felt
like a crime.

"What if you meet Prince Charming and you're married to me?" Logan asked.

She pretended to be aghast. "What? You're not Prince Charming? And here I thought I had finally found him."

Logan pulled her close, brushing a strand of hair off her face that the ocean breeze tried to push back again.

"I'd make a defective husband."

"You think I'm crazy and are trying to let me down easy."

"No, I think you're crazy-kind and crazy-generous and crazy-immensely-caring, and I'm wondering how I was lucky enough to meet you."

"Is that a yes? Because if it is I need you to sign a prenuptial agreement."

He looked surprised. Why was she still talking? Why was she still pushing this idea so hard?

She laughed and lunged at him, trying to play her way past the hurt at his rejection. He'd clued in at how nuts (or desperate) she must be to offer to break the law for him—a stranger. But he was too quick, swinging her past him as she moved forward, then collecting her in his arms, giving her a quick hug she knew was him expressing a surplus of gratitude. Even if he thought she was crazy.

"You might be cute, but you don't get the shop I spent fifteen years saving up to buy."

"You've been saving since you were ten?" He tipped his head back, smiling at her.

"I'm thirty-one, thank you very much. But you *can* have my debt."

"Are you sure?"

"It's a pretty sizable gift, but I think I could find the generosity of spirit in order to give it to you."

She met his warm gaze. She hated that he and Annabelle could become separated. Marriage was such an easy answer and it hurt nobody.

"You sure?" he repeated.

"One condition."

Logan nodded.

"Absolutely no lies. You have to be totally honest with me. About everything."

LOGAN WAS GETTING WHAT HE NEEDED—what he wanted. He could stay on the case, remain close to Annabelle.

But that meant deceiving Ginger on a whole new level and putting her closer to danger. It also meant he had to break his first promise as a truly engaged man—no lying.

He'd managed to play it cool, though, as Ginger laid out a plan for them. He'd hid his desperation, his relief, letting her push the idea, so she wouldn't back out later.

Marriage solved everything.

And he was getting married. To Ginger.

Tonight.

"We want to cash in our elopement wedding," Ginger said, bustling up to guest services. It was minutes before they closed and she smacked the signed contract on the desk next to the woman's cinnamon bun, sending the large potted plants on either end of the large marble surface waving. "Tonight."

The middle-aged woman blinked once, twice. "Tonight?"

"Yes, please, Zoe." Ginger leaned closer, her body language confiding, and Logan took the opportunity to admire the way her capris hugged her hips. "Did you call Ash? He's supercute."

Zoe nodded and smiled, fingering the contract. "We chatted for an hour."

"Really?" Ginger looked tickled pink.

"We're going out on Friday night."

"That's so great!"

"But the elopement?" Zoe happy expression faded. "We need time to prepare."

"It's an elopement," Ginger replied said carefully, and Logan fought a smile. She'd made up her mind and that was it. Off she went to save his world, fix his problems.

If he hurt her in any way he was pretty sure he'd never forgive himself.

He tried to focus on his past training. A little heartbreak collateral was nothing compared to the lives he could save by putting Vito behind bars. It was more about what she'd feel when she found out that everything about him other than Annabelle—the only good thing in his life—was a big, fat, ugly lie.

Not that she'd ever learn he was a liar, a spy. He needed to focus on that. It was his job to weave the whole story from start to finish so she'd never learn the truth. He would protect her, allow her to remain fine, unaffected, good to go live her life, believing she'd done something beneficial for a family. Because that's what AnnaBee was. Family.

He didn't know where his next mission would take him, but he hoped it wouldn't be far from her. He found himself frowning, arms crossed. He just kept finding more problems to solve, didn't he? He couldn't even enjoy the fact that this curvaceous, kindhearted woman cared enough to commit fraud?

Then again, he'd kind of liked her argument about how it couldn't possibly be against the law, since they were the good guys.

Ginger was watching him uncertainly and he realized he was scowling. Not something the groom-to-be should be doing.

"Sorry." He adjusted his expression. "I was worrying about Annabelle."

"Well, after tonight you won't have to worry any longer." Her smile brightened and, like the hundred-watt beam that it was, lit up his world.

"Thanks." He tipped her head toward him, planting a kiss in her auburn curls.

She was a good woman and he hoped whoever found her after him loved her in all the ways she deserved.

"Zoe is going to set things up. Our wedding will be something simple. Okay?" Ginger waved a few papers at him. "And they have prenup templates. We just fill one in and their legal team makes it fancy and official."

"Perfect." Logan drew her close, lowering his lips to hers, kissing her with time and care. Before long, the kiss heated like always, leaving him reckless and aroused, the usual guard he kept between him and others gone.

"What are we going to wear?" she whispered when they'd broken free.

All he could imagine was her birthday suit. He'd bet she had freckles in unexpected places. "There's a boutique down the beach. Something beachy?"

Within minutes they were in a thatch-roofed hut, Ginger's

arm piled with clothes to try on. "My grandmother is going to kill me."

"Why's that?" He pulled a pair of casual slacks and a button-up shirt off the rack. He already had something like it back at the cottage, but figured he got married only once. Well, twice. And since this one was just part of his cover, probably thrice.

He'd better not spend a lot.

"The store..." She gave him a meaningful look.

"Oh, right. Bridal thing back home."

"Wanda's Wedding Store—I'm going to rename it to Veils and Vows."

"I like that."

"Me, too." She gave him one of those big smiles of hers. "The shop is among the best in the state."

"Why don't you wear your green dress?" he asked, looking at the garments in her arms. They were all loose, white numbers you'd expect in a beach wedding, and he knew they wouldn't be nearly as sexy as the emerald dress she'd been wearing the night they'd met. Last night. Wow. Time flew while on a mission.

She contemplated the pile of cotton. "I guess..."

He grabbed the clothes from her, dumping them on a nearby chair along with his own chosen outfit. "As much as I'd love to watch you play dress-up, I think you already own something much sexier." Besides, he knew she was on a budget, and she didn't need to spend money on him— especially since he was fairly certain she wouldn't let him pay.

Back at the cottage, as Ginger shut the door behind them, the breeze caught it, sending it shut with a bang. Logan heard a clatter in the bathroom that sounded a lot like his Beretta falling from its hiding spot, thanks to the way the cottage shook with the slam.

"What was that?" she asked.

"I'll check it out." He was across the room in seconds, Ginger on his heels. She gasped when she saw the handgun lying on the bathroom floor.

"Well. Huh." He scratched his head as if he was confused. "I guess some places leave guns as well as chocolates. The roaches must be bad."

Ginger was clinging to his shoulder. "Is someone in there? Check the tub."

He could see from his spot that there was nobody in the Jacuzzi nor behind the door. It was his gun. That simple.

"It's clear."

"You sure?" She was trembling, and he placed the weapon on the counter before turning to face her.

"Ginger, whenever you're with me, you're safe. You understand? Always."

She swallowed hard.

The wind rattled the shutters against the side of the cottage and she clung closer.

He stroked her cheek, tipping her face to his. "I promise."

She nodded slowly.

Knowing he shouldn't, he kissed her. Her arms swept around his shoulders, her legs lifting as she hoisted herself into his arms. She felt so good, wrapped around him, and he spun, gently pressing her to the wall, deepening the kiss. The act unleashed her, her kisses turning frantic.

Her lips were everywhere as he allowed his hand to drift up her side, cupping her soft curves. He moaned into her mouth, knowing he was losing a grip on reality, his surroundings. But for once in his life he didn't care.

THANK GOODNESS FOR THE COTTAGES' on-site handyman, Jace Fisher, or Ginger would have taken that heavy petting session a bit too far for two people about to jump into a marriage of convenience with nothing more than...a newly forged friendship as a base. And lust. There was definitely some of that going around.

The man had knocked, sending Ginger to the floor as Logan hurried to the window to peek out before answering the door. He'd relaxed immediately, but still had that ever-alert, protective edge to him. Instead of it making her nervous, as she would have predicted, it actually made her feel safe.

The two men chatted, Jace letting Logan know what he was up to, while Ginger took the opportunity to slow her racing heart and go in search of her shirt. She'd barely noticed that it had come off, her focus being solely on Logan.

He'd been completely unfazed by the gun lying on the bathroom floor—likely another result of his army training. It was still on the counter and that made her slightly nervous. What else was hiding in the cottage? And why would anyone carry a weapon while staying in a honeymoon cottage? The idea of the two together left her feeling shaky inside, vulnerable.

But then Logan...he'd just swept her up and stared at her with those steady gray eyes, telling her that as long as she was with him she'd be safe. And she'd felt it. Felt how much he meant the words, felt his honesty, the truth.

And that made her head go crazy, her heart start to sway in his direction despite her mental reminders telling it not to. Logan was a man she could just...

Lose herself in.

And so part of her was relieved for Jace's timing.

But part of her wasn't.

Logan came inside again, his back to the door. He paused, watching her.

She didn't know what to do. Stare back? Find an outfit for their upcoming wedding? Say something like "you're the best kisser I've ever met in my entire life and part of me is hoping we'll consummate this fake marriage we're heading into"?

His own decision apparently made, Logan strode toward her. In seconds he had taken her in his arms again, kissing her in that slow, sweet, intense way that sent her down a rabbit hole where there was nothing but the two of them falling into each other.

CHAPTER 4

Logan Stone stood beside Ginger McGinty, prepared to lie.

Cherish. Honor. Protect.

He could do those things.

It was the love and not hurt her part that was going to be tricky.

He'd stood like this once before, uttering those very words. Making promises. He'd thought he could keep them the first time, a total no-brainer. This time he hoped he could keep at least half of them without turning into his wife's worst enemy. He needed to do his best to let her keep living the fantasy of a guy trying to do the right thing for Annabelle.

And he'd have to keep their contact short. He hadn't been able to hold on to Kristy, because she'd seen the real him. If Ginger ever did, she'd definitely leave, unbelievably hurt. And he knew she had the potential to, because she already saw parts of him that nobody else had noticed. But if she ever saw Logan the dangerous spy she could blow everything, including her own heart.

But that was merely collateral, he reminded himself. He had to be ruthless. He had a new visa application to make, a yacht to bug, a bad guy to catch.

Keep the woman safe, then disappear.

Except she knew where Annabelle lived.

Everywhere he looked...problems.

The ocean breeze blew Ginger's loose curls around her shoulders and she was smiling softly as she repeated her set of vows. He had rarely seen her face without a smile on it. She deserved a happily ever after. She was happy, warm, kind and wonderful. Trusting.

What could be so broken in her life that she thought marrying him was a good deal?

He brushed her cheek with his fingertips, overcome by a feeling of protectiveness. He wished he could be everything she deserved. Wished somehow...

He was acting sentimental. It was the vows, the flowers, the whole "until death do you part" business.

He wasn't that man. He was a ruthless spy on a mission. The marriage he was entering into was as fake as his undercover name, Logan Stone.

Their marriage would be null and void before they even said "I do." It would never be fraud because it wasn't a real marriage. Yes, the new visa would go through, because his paperwork was that good. But there was no real Logan Stone even though everyone from Annabelle to nosy Lucille knew him as such. Ginger's new husband would never be more than a ghost.

Ginger was steady, watching him quietly, her hands in his now.

They shared their I do's and Logan blinked back the unnecessary emotion. She was a good citizen unknowingly helping him catch a bad guy.

But man, she could kiss like a fiend, make him forget

everything he was trained to do. He was already jealous of the guy who would come along after him. He hoped he deserved her. Hoped he was everything Logan tried to be: kind, caring, thoughtful.

They were pronounced husband and wife and she gave a half smile of disbelief. "That was easy," she said.

Crime committed. Just like that. Well, an almost-crime, seeing as she'd only married his cover.

He hoped Ginger's grandmother wasn't the type to track him down and beat him with her purse for sneaking her granddaughter into an elopement. He'd met a woman like that in Mumbai and his head hurt just thinking about that swinging handbag.

"Kiss me, Logan."

Logan glanced around. The beach. The flowers, the arch. The witnesses, Ted and Nadia. A few staff.

Right. Married.

To the most beautiful, captivating woman. The only person who could bring him down, defeat him, at the same time as lifting him up, letting him breathe, letting him live once again like a real man, a real person.

All he had to do was seal the deal with a kiss, show her how special she really was.

Easy.

$\sim$

LOGAN SWEPT GINGER INTO A KISS that didn't hold back in the way his others had, and she did her best to hold on, to not pass out from the sheer passionate appreciation she had for his muscular form pressing against her while kissing the living daylights out of her.

They broke the kiss, amid cheers from Nadia and Ted.

"You're going to have to carry me," Ginger said dramatically, sagging in Logan's arms.

He chuckled and said with a growl, "I'll make sure you can't walk for a day."

Ginger felt herself blush, wondering if his words were a promise or merely part of their show. She half wished it was the former.

"Logan, do you have a brother I could meet?" Nadia joked from her nearby spot on the beach.

"Hey," her fiancé protested.

Laughing, Nadia hooked her arm through Ginger's, leading her toward the dinner table set up on the beach nearby, whispering about how hunky Logan was.

Oh, her body didn't need anyone telling her—it already knew. That kiss...it had been...well, she didn't have words, just blown circuits.

Her husband could kiss like nobody she'd ever met.

Her *husband*.

Wow, did she ever like the sound of that rolling around in her head.

But what was she going to tell her grandmother? Her parents? Blueberry Springs? Nobody would believe the stories. Nobody would believe he was real.

He was her secret. She didn't have many, but rather often kept them for others such as the doozy between her hometown friend Devon Mattson and her old college roommate Olivia Carrington. Their secret went back to their college days and had played out not too far from Indigo Bay.

Over the years Ginger hadn't let even a telltale flutter of her eyelashes hint to others that she knew something about Devon's past which kept him from settling down despite the best efforts of Blueberry Springs matchmakers.

But this new secret was big, hers, and well within the league of her father's. That idea hit her hard, taking the joy from her smile.

She should have thought about home first, Logan second.

She hadn't changed, had she? She was still rushing into things, seeing only the good, not the reality of the situation. How was she ever going to have her happily ever after if she kept choosing the wrong men? Just look at her. Now she was hitched to a guy who would need to keep her married to him for two to three years if he planned on applying for a green card.

What if she found someone else and wanted to get married and start a family? It could be too late by the time she and Logan ended things.

She hadn't thought it through. She'd just jumped in, clinging to the romantic idea of keeping his family together.

And yet rushing into things felt different this time. Was it because it wasn't love and she wasn't falling for him? Because the entire agreement was that they would use each other, then end it when they had what they needed—what he needed?

She knew that wasn't it. This whatever it was with Logan felt more solid than anything else, had which made no sense.

Ginger paused at the small table strewn with flower petals, the candles set in jeweled jars flickering in the light ocean breeze that made its way past a trellis thick with red roses that protected them from the Atlantic. There were four seats

—for her, Logan and their two guests. When Logan held out her chair, allowing her to sit, he trailed his fingers across her shoulder blades like a promise.

Champagne was poured and fresh bread sticks brought out.

Logan was watching her, noticing her quiet mood. He reached out, giving her hand a squeeze.

Ginger focused on her Caesar salad, smiling at the right times in Nadia's stories. Logan had requested steak and potatoes, and Ginger was grateful for something more solid to chew when her salad was done so she didn't have to think, because inside she was panicking.

What had she done?

She'd met Logan only yesterday! Twenty-four hours ago.

A teenaged boy stopped at their table, his golf shirt sporting the name of the cottages.

"Avery, my man!" Logan gave him a funny guy-to-guy handshake and Ginger felt her heart grow a size bigger. Logan was a good man. That's why she'd married him.

Married.

That still packed a wallop though, didn't it?

"How did the math test go?" Logan asked.

"Aced it." The boy gave a sheepish, proud smile. "Did you get married?"

Logan reached for Ginger's hand, leaning closer. "Sure did. Ginger, this is Avery, the math ace. Avery, my beautiful wife, Ginger." He kissed her hand, giving her a lingering look that had heat pooling in places it shouldn't while out in public. Their earlier kisses had been hot, taking them close to the proverbial edge, and she had a feeling neither of them would be able to hold back much longer.

But was she ready to give this marriage legitimacy by consummating it? She wasn't entirely sure.

"Cool." Avery bobbed his head a few times.

A woman who looked to be in her seventies, despite her blond hair, joined Avery. She presented herself like a full Southern belle, with her fitted dress, high heels and perfect hair. Ginger was immediately intrigued.

"Hello, Avery. Logan." The woman sized up Ginger, the new rings on her finger as well as Logan's. She turned her attention to Logan, looking unimpressed. "And now you're married?"

"I told you I was engaged." He winked at the woman, who harrumphed.

"I had a very nice woman lined up for you, you know."

Logan turned to Ginger. "Lucille was hoping to set me up on a blind date with her great-niece."

Ginger bit back her amusement at the woman's obvious displeasure over being taken out of the match-up game. "Sorry."

Lucille narrowed her eyes at them suspiciously as though trying to sniff out the reason for their hurried nuptials.

"Well, I have to get back to work," Avery said, looking uncomfortable.

Lucille gave another harrumph and left, too, after claiming that she knew what Logan was up to.

As soon as they were out of earshot, Nadia leaned forward, asking, "Who's Avery?"

"I tutor him in math sometimes. Good kid."

"Don't you just love Logan?" Nadia asked Ginger. She had one elbow on the table as she gaped openly at him, and

Ginger felt a flash of jealousy even though she knew Nadia would never stray from Ted and vice versa.

"I'm right here," her fiancé teased. "And if I'd known you found math cool I would have told you about what a math-lete I was in school."

Nadia slipped her hand onto his thigh. "What's a math-lete?"

"An athlete. In math." Ted gave a chuckle. "I was a nerd, hon. Full out."

Nadia leaned over to give him a kiss. "That's part of what I love so much about you. You're good with money, knowing where to invest and when, too. Plus you're good in bed."

The two of them laughed.

"So what drew *you* two together?" Ted asked, waving his champagne flute toward Ginger and Logan.

"Besides running into each other," Nadia added, recalling their story from the night before.

Ginger looked at Logan and bit her bottom lip. How truthful should she be?

"My first wife couldn't see the real me," Logan said. "Ginger can."

Ginger paused, pressing her hand against her chest. His words felt so...

Logan looked lost as he took another sip of his drink. "That was a poor comparison, wasn't it? Kinda like whacking a baby kanga at a kid's birthday party."

Ginger gave his hand a squeeze. "That, right there. That's what drew me to Logan."

Nadia sat back in her chair with a frown. "Whacking baby animals?"

"No," Ginger said softly. "That little flare of real man

hiding under the bulk. You're not who you say you are, Logan Stone, and I'm going to figure you out."

∞

GINGER WAS DOING IT AGAIN. That look-inside-his-soul thing she did, pinning him with her gaze. She knew he wasn't who he pretended to be, but he didn't think she had figured out who he really was.

Unless *she* wasn't who *she* said she was...

What if she was a spy for Vito? A henchman?

And he'd just married her.

Logan fought with himself, struggling to keep his hand under hers, act like a man who wasn't quickly shutting down the outside world, putting himself in a bunker so he could protect himself, have a good think.

Ginger laughed, watching him. "I'm freaking you out, aren't I?" She leaned closer, running her fingers through his hair in a way that sent shivers down his spine like rockets. "You're so used to hiding you don't know what to do with a woman who sees you, do you?"

He fell into the depths of her emerald eyes—eyes that sometimes looked almost gray like his own, but today looked just as bright as her dress. Sharp eyes. Eyes that saw everything. And yet there was an innocence, a fresh look at life that agents no longer possessed after about five months on the job. And that spark? He'd never met a true villain with that, either.

She was one of a kind or else who she truly was—just a woman. Someone he could hide behind while angling closer to a man who killed out of greed.

He forgot about their tablemates, Nadia and Ted, as he focused on Ginger, mindlessly nodding his approval when Dallas, the resort owner, came by to see that all was to their satisfaction. Ginger had grown quiet since saying their vows, and he believed she was experiencing doubts.

"And who are you?" he asked, dragging his finger across her palm.

Her back straightened and she let out a shaky breath. "Your wife."

She bit her bottom lip as though trying to mask her delight with his touch and attention, but the intensity in her green eyes had ratcheted up to another level. A level he wouldn't mind exploring.

Ginger McGinty was different from the rest, and not just because she cared and mattered. Darn it, but she saw the man he was trying to be, and that made him feel like his whole world could change, that this fake marriage could turn out differently than they'd planned.

But it was built upon a bed of lies. Because once he peeked out from under them, she'd see what a big liar and user he had been from the moment they'd met, and that would be it. Game over. Girl gone.

Devastation.

Because of him.

The very idea made it difficult to breathe.

Nadia and Ted pushed their chairs back, quietly saying good-night, slipping off so as not to break the spell between the newlyweds.

"Do you trust me?" Logan asked Ginger, still stroking her hand.

She watched him, those eyes probing. "I think I do."

"But you're not sure?"

She tilted her head to the side. "I don't actually know you that well."

"I had a dog named Ribbit as a kid, and my favorite color is the color of your eyes."

She blushed, looking away.

"I know that you aren't used to compliments. You like them but you don't want to depend on them, believe them."

"What makes you so smart?"

"Life."

"Do you trust *me*?" she asked, shifting closer.

"Yes."

"No hesitation?" She seemed surprised.

"I have a pretty good sense about people."

"Then what am I thinking right now?"

He lifted a strawberry from the fruit platter that had been delivered between the main course and the cake. He held it to her mouth and she took a bite. "I didn't say I was a mind reader," he claimed.

"I don't know what to think about you."

He did his best not to pull back, put up his guard, because he knew she'd see it.

"You're all tough and burly. Manly. But you're also squishy-sweet."

Logan frowned, unsure whether she'd just delivered a compliment or not. "Don't tell my personal trainer that."

"You have a personal trainer?"

"No."

"See? How can I fully trust a man when I don't even know if he has a trainer?"

"A trainer makes me trustworthy?"

She shook her head. "You're deliberately obtuse."

"You're deliberately cute." He tapped the end of her nose.

"What are we going to do, Logan?" Her eyes were pleading, her fears coming to the surface.

"We're going to hold on and see where we are by the time you have to return home." He paused, caressing her hand. "Because the past twenty-four hours have been simply unreal and I think it's shown us that we can't escape destiny."

$\sim$

"THAT WAS NICE," GINGER SAID AS they walked back along the beach. There was cheering up ahead, tiki torches lighting up the darkened beach, the full moon hiding behind a few clouds. Her best guess was that it was the engaged couples' games night.

"Are we still allowed to join in now that we're married?" she wondered aloud. It would be a shame if the two of them no longer got to go. Although lately she'd been less eager to pick everyone's brains about the shop, and more interested in spending time with Logan.

It would be wise to return her focus to work, the whole reason she'd traveled all this way.

"Hmm?" Logan looked up. They'd taken turns being quiet and introspective tonight, and she wondered if their wedding had brought back memories of his first wife.

He caught her hand, drawing it to his lips, kissing her knuckles, suddenly back from wherever his mind had wandered to. "Nice rings."

"Thanks. I know a guy."

"Yeah?"

"Yeah... Want to join the fun?" she asked. She wasn't in a rush to go back to their cottage, where she was certain staff had decked out the place, expecting them to consummate their union like true newlyweds would.

Sure, it wouldn't be a heartbreak to make love with Logan, but she also didn't want to get attached, like the big sucker she was. Ginger could already feel herself being pulled in. If they acted like a married couple both in and out of the cottage, well, she worried her heart might wake up, shed its mourning clothes and hop on in without realizing this wasn't serious or real.

Logan was already drawing her toward the rowdy group of lovers, intent on joining them.

"What are they doing?" she asked, trying to make sense of the hubbub.

"Looks like the limbo."

"I rock the limbo."

He gave her an appraising look. "In that dress?"

"In anything." Feeling playful, Ginger hiked the skirt of her dress a little higher and acted like she was going under a limbo stick. "See?"

"Sexy."

"You haven't seen anything yet," she said with a wink.

Moments later they were among the throng of people and pushed onto a small stage strewn with roses for an upcoming game. Logan scooped up a rose and handed it to Ginger.

The game organizer had them face each other before drilling them with questions. The goal was to answer more than any other couple in one minute.

"Close your eyes, Logan and Ginger."

They complied.

"What's your lover's eye color?"

"Green," snapped Logan.

"Gray with flecks of yellow," Ginger said.

"Open your eyes. Correct! First fight."

"Haven't had one." They smiled at each other.

"None?" The organizer looked out at the crowd, many of whom jeered in disbelief.

"Ginger, your dream for Logan."

"That he returns to Blueberry Springs with me."

She inhaled sharply. Shoot. Where had that come from? Even Logan's eyebrows shot up, but before she could think on it, the next question was being asked.

"Logan? Same question."

"That she stays safe."

The crowd gave a soft "aw..."

There was his safety thing again. Maybe the gun from their cottage had been his. But if so, why not fess up?

"How many kids?"

"Ten," Ginger said, and Logan laughed. "I mean one. I don't know!" The pressure of an immediate answer was starting to unwind her ability to think before speaking.

Logan said, "How about two or three?"

"Perfect."

"Sexiest thing about each other?"

"Everything," Ginger said breathily, before catching herself and giggling.

"I'd agree," Logan said. He ran a hand down her bare arm, taking her in. Time slowed and all that mattered was the man in front of her. Her husband.

"Pick one thing," the announcer insisted.

"His caring side."

Logan stared at her hard enough that she worried she'd said the wrong thing.

"Her faith and trust in me," he replied finally. He pulled Ginger into a soft kiss and she felt herself begin to fall.

CHAPTER 5

Logan swam through the Atlantic, his flippers pushing him forward as he passed clumps of seaweed and the odd school of speckled sea trout. The moon was bright, giving him enough light he didn't need his own if he stayed near the surface. When he reached the marina he made a silent wish that Ginger would continue as his talisman.

He didn't like the water in marinas. Not just because boat owners occasionally forgot to close the valve on their black tanks when they came in from deeper waters, but because he was never fully trusting of marina ground fault protection systems, which were meant to protect anyone in the water from being electrocuted by the cables running power to the docks.

He moved through the water, counting off docks until he came to the one that had Vito's yacht. He'd placed a tracking device on it a month ago, but the boat had been pulled out of the water for maintenance and it had been knocked off along with the barnacles.

Logan pulled the new tracker from his belt and, with gloved hands, attached it to the boat's hull.

Task completed, he began the long swim back to Ginger.

Ginger. She thought he was caring. That's what she'd said at the party hours earlier. Caring. Him.

The woman who saw him. The woman who had ensured he now had access to a visa, giving him time to finish the mission, plus come up with a new plan for himself and Annabelle.

But Ginger...

Sweet, sweet Ginger.

The two of them had slipped out of the party and walked back to their cottage in silence. They'd changed into their pajamas and wordlessly cuddled on the giant bed among the candles and flowers, drifting off to sleep.

He'd never done that before. Just been with someone. Quiet. Together. Bonded on a level that required nothing, not even words.

It had been difficult pulling himself out of bed and into the cold waters of the Atlantic. And just as difficult to keep pushing aside the dream she'd blurted out. She wanted him to come home with her.

It didn't fit. And yet...he kept thinking about it, imagining it, wondering what it would be like to step back into civilian life, to marry, to allow himself to have dreams of a family once again.

He let himself mull over what the changes in his recent thinking might mean in regards to his job, before switching his mind back to the mission. Tomorrow he'd dress as a maintenance worker and add eyes and ears onboard Vito's yacht, something he hadn't done yet due to work on its interior. Bugging devices were, of course, already in Vito's car and beach house, and regular intel was downloaded by the agency. So far nothing convicting, but he was getting there and had high hopes for Thursday.

Nearing the cottages, Logan checked his watch: 3:48 a.m. Not bad. He was still in that quiet window of the night. Late enough that most partyers had already found their way home, and early enough the morning staff weren't heading in to work yet. He would come ashore, ditch the gear—putting it back in the resort's scuba shed—then slip into bed alongside the woman who was slowly worming her way into his life.

Logan swam into shallow waters, surfacing once, checking the beach for eyes. This was where the full moon above was both a blessing and a curse. Blessing because he could see what he was up against, curse because it meant he was almost as easy to spot.

Seeing the coast was clear, he swam in as shallow as his gear would allow, then surfaced. He stood, turning so his back was to the shore and the rows of cute cottages lining the beach, then waded backward in the rolling waves so his flippers wouldn't catch. The night was beautiful, the moon's reflection rippling on the ocean swells. It was a nice night to be out for a swim. With everything so quiet and calm it made it difficult to believe a diamond smuggler lived on these very shores.

Logan stepped onto the firm wet sand of the beach and turned to take off his flippers.

"What do you think you're doing?"

He stumbled, digging one his flippers in the sand and tumbling over.

"Ginger!"

She stood above him, hands on her hips, looking very

much the wife of a man caught scuba diving alone, in the middle of the night.

Uh-oh.

"Hi, honey."

"Don't 'hi honey' me."

May as well go with the truth.

"This is exactly what it looks like."

"Really?" She didn't sound convinced, but his honesty had taken her edge and disintegrated it.

"Yup. And you look beautiful in the moonlight."

"Scuba diving? In the middle of the night?"

He slipped off the flippers. "It's just around supper in Australia."

"That's not going to work with me, buster." She pulled him to his feet and he was half tempted to resist, give her a gentle tug that would have her landing on top of him in her jeans and sweatshirt. "You didn't tell anyone where you were going."

"Sorry."

She shook her head, gazing up at him. "You do weird things in the middle of the night."

"True."

She was studying him, obviously wishing she had the right to interrogate him. Instead of pursuing the thread of conversation like most women would have, she gave up with a sigh. "How did you even find a wetsuit to fit you?"

She was appraising him now, her curiosity palpable. The suit was thick and tight, no doubt showcasing everything he had to offer, the moonlight enhancing certain bulges as the wet material gleamed. He stood a little taller.

"Want to help me take it off?" he asked. His voice was

lower, his tone slightly gruff as he tried to hide his longing for the woman before him.

"Ha," she said weakly.

"Please?" He turned, offering her his back, where the zipper was located. It appeased him knowing she felt the draw, too. That pull cord that seemed connected to the shutter they both usually kept closed around others. Around her the shutters opened and she walked right on in without the usual sirens blaring or lasers slicing the air. It was like she had the top-secret, high-clearance fingerprint that allowed her exclusive entry. He kind of liked the idea of that. Having someone who belonged, who fitted up against his soul.

As she helped him out of the suit, moving around to face him, her cool fingers brushed his warm skin. She peeled the rubber wetsuit down his shoulders, his hands still pinned in the tight cuffs.

"I think I'll tickle you," she declared, taking a step closer, fingers drifting like seaweed over his exposed flesh as she decided on her best approach. He flung his hands out at his sides, pulling them free of the sleeves as he hustled backward.

"Oh, no." He had never been ticklish, as he hated the helpless feeling it gave him, being at someone else's mercy. And yet the very idea of her trying to tickle him made him weak, his body betraying him, his laughter already free of the gates. He stumbled backward into the softer, deeper sand, tumbling to the ground once more, reduced to laughter. "I'm *not* ticklish. Seriously."

"Man, you are just too easy. I barely even touched you," she said.

Apparently feeling generous, she resisted attacking him and helped him doff the rest of his suit.

"Next time wake me up and I'll go with you," she said, holding the utility belt for him.

"You know how to scuba?"

"No, but I like mischief and I can tell you were up to some."

He stilled, more curious than alarmed. "Can you?"

"Yes." She knelt beside him, tugging the clingy neoprene layer from around his ankles. After the snug warmth of the suit, the cool night air felt cold against his skin. It made him feel alive, and he reached for Ginger, tugging her to the sand beside him. He rolled onto his side, sheltering her.

She was quiet, aware.

He brushed a lock of hair from her cheek, then her forehead.

He wished time would stand still, his enemies already fallen. He wished he could tell her that her good deed was going to help more than just himself and Annabelle. Ginger was someone who should never doubt herself, because her instincts were solid, her joy unrivaled. He wished he could let her know that when he slipped away, it was because he didn't want to hurt her.

GINGER HELD HER HUSBAND'S HAND and climbed aboard Vito's yacht, Nadia and Ted following on their heels. The past two days had been a blur of workshops, enjoying the Southern hospitality dinner that they'd won—it had been absolutely fabulous—and picking the brains of other couples, as well as spending as much time as she could with Logan.

Although now it was time to start dialing it back, in

preparation for going home. Logan wasn't coming to Blueberry Springs—he was leaving their marriage behind as he fulfilled his commitments to Annabelle, while Ginger returned to her real life. A life that looked so dull in comparison to the fun and playful time she'd had here. In two days she would be going home and would likely never see Logan, her husband, again. It was an odd feeling, and in a way she already missed him, which she knew was silly. She was already in too deep and was only going to have her heart broken if she allowed herself to continue to fall.

Impulsively, she turned on the large boat's deck and wrapped her arms around Logan's waist, holding him closer. She'd been honest when she'd blurted out that she wanted him to follow her back to Blueberry Springs. Even though she knew he couldn't, she still wished it, wanting to see what might happen between them.

But that wasn't his choice, even if being with him felt like the best, most natural thing she'd ever experienced. Maybe it was simply because there was no pressure to impress him for fear that he would leave, because it would be her who was going this time.

"Follow my lead today," Logan whispered against her ear, and her heart gave a little jump in her chest. She glanced up, unable to prevent the hope that welled inside her whenever they touched. He placed a kiss on her cheek and smiled, but she could see the tension riding in his jaw. He'd been edgy since dawn, pulling away from her more often than not. Logan had secrets, that she knew. Secrets he wasn't sharing with her, and she had to remind herself that it was because they weren't really married, weren't really each other's confidants, despite saying they trusted each other.

They would be parting soon.

"Are you doing—" Before she could finish asking if he was doing all right, he tipped his head down, capturing her mouth in a kiss so hot she nearly asked if there was a spare room aboard that they could borrow.

"You sure can kiss," she said breathlessly when they broke apart. He gave her a distracted smile and she swallowed hard and slipped out of his grasp.

She shouldn't take his behavior personally. His first wife had left him, and Ginger was leaving him in two days. She knew what being left felt like.

They listened as the captain gave a speech on safety, pointing out the lifejackets and other flotation devices. She half listened, more curious about Logan and what she could do to get him to open up to her again.

Vito and his slender wife welcomed everyone aboard when the captain finished, and the yacht set sail, increasing Logan's unease.

"You don't like sailing?" Ginger asked him, relieved to have possibly found the source of his odd behavior. He kept looking around, as though mentally doing a head count on a kindergarten field trip.

"Yeah."

For days she hadn't pried whenever he pulled back, but today she wanted to sneak her way into that part of him he kept reserved. That part she couldn't quite see all the way into. The part that reminded her that even though she might be falling for him, it wasn't something he wanted, because of whatever it was he had in that locked box inside him.

"Logan, what's wrong?"

He finally met her eyes, his own filled with what looked like worry. He took her hand, holding it firmly.

"Ginger, no matter what..." He did a visual check of the other passengers again before returning his gaze to her. "What we have here? It's real."

She felt heat flood her as he confirmed her feelings as his own.

"It does feel real, doesn't it?" Did that scare him?

"And anything I say or do is about *me*. Not you."

"Is this about your first wife?" Her warm feeling had vanished, turning into the cold one she got before a man broke up with her.

Stupid heart, falling for Logan.

"No, not at all."

"Are you breaking up with me?"

He blinked twice. "What? No. I care for you. A lot."

Ginger's tension melted. "Really?"

He inhaled slowly before letting his breath out again. "Yeah."

He said that like it was a problem. But still. He liked her. She didn't need more than that at the moment.

She smiled and hugged him tight. "Me, too."

He was stiff in her arms, not letting go in the way she expected. He patted her head uncertainly, then pushed her back. "Whatever happens today, just trust me, okay? Know that you know the real me."

She frowned. "Logan, is something—"

"Just promise you'll trust me." His voice was lower, more urgent now. "And do whatever I ask you to without questioning it."

"Uh, is there a safe word?" she joked. "I'm not really into

the dominance-submissive thing. I mean, I'm a bit curious, but—"

He didn't smile, didn't laugh. She was with a whole new Logan. The one she hadn't ever managed to unearth. Until now. And she wasn't sure how to take it. He had a ruthless look in his gaze, a resolve so steely it frightened her. This wasn't the man she'd expected to find.

"Promise," he commanded.

"Okay. Okay, I promise," she said quickly, feeling the need for more space. She glanced out at the shore, which was rapidly growing distant. Ginger had a feeling she knew her husband of two and a half days even less than she'd believed.

$\sim$

NEVER FALL IN LOVE ON THE JOB—that was the rule. And what had he done? Fallen for Ginger McGinty. The idea of her here on the yacht with a man who killed anyone who stood in his way, or knew too much, was driving Logan out of his mind.

What if something happened? What if Ginger figured things out and spoke up? What if Vito's men knew who Logan was and tipped him overboard, then took off with Ginger and hurt her?

The idea had him clutching the side rail, his stomach tight.

"Are you okay?" Ginger tentatively touched his shoulder. He'd scared her an hour ago, he knew. He had let his fear for her overcome him.

But he had to know she would obey, that she would do whatever he needed her to in order to remain safe, because he sure couldn't tell her who he was—not without losing his job. And then who would he be? There wasn't much need for ruthless men outside of spy agencies and those cage fights his agent pal Zach Forrester sometimes watched.

It was hardly fair, scaring her, but Logan knew how far south "meetings" could go, and everyone on board was a puzzle piece Vito needed to unload his dirty diamonds. Logan was a wholesaler who could mix them with clean diamonds. A stone setter was sitting beside Ted, who was a chain store owner. And they were all about to become cogs in Vito's new deal.

If Ginger asked him what his biggest fear was today, Logan would say it was that he might not be able to keep her safe in the moment she needed him most.

He should have found a way to leave her behind.

He'd mixed real life and the mission, and that made him a horrible agent. Add in that he'd put a civilian at risk as part of his cover.

In his books, that was unforgivable.

"Logan?" She was worried about him; he could hear it in her voice.

"Yeah, fine."

He hated himself. It was that simple.

He'd lost his edge as an agent, and he'd be lucky if the whole mission didn't backfire as a result.

He straightened, unable to look at Ginger, see her as someone who was vulnerable, innocent and about to become a part of something that was most definitely not.

What Ginger had seen and loved about him was fake. It was part of the act, an act that had begun to feel more real than who he truly was.

He felt like Logan Stone, diamond wholesaler. Kind, caring

and thoughtful. A man who volunteered and acted as though he had all the elements of a real man.

But in truth, he was nothing more than a ruthless agent trained to take care of the world's dirty underbelly. And when pure and innocent Ginger saw that later on today, she'd recoil. When she saw the lies, it would be over. The man she was falling for did not truly exist, no matter how much Logan wanted him to.

He shut his eyes. In another world, another time...he could maybe try to become the man she saw. The man he wanted to be.

But not today.

Today he had to be the man who brought down a diamond smuggler.

GINGER DIDN'T KNOW WHAT TO THINK. Logan and she had such tender moments where everything felt real, like their souls touched. Then others when he withdrew and shut her out.

He was a good man, but something wasn't right. There was something unknown bubbling under the surface and it scared her.

She excused herself to use the washroom, leaving him at the rail, where he was silently cursing himself.

Yeah, she got it. He couldn't do it any longer. He'd been lying and it was time to cut the cord.

She'd had such high hopes for today. She'd planned to enjoy the sun and Logan, savor her freedom to just be, before she had to return home to the endless job of running her own business. She loved it, she did. But it felt flat, knowing she'd be there without him.

She was a fool. She'd skipped out on a workshop she'd paid to attend, in order to be here with Logan, because she'd believed. Believed in fairy tales, obviously.

Now she wanted to be back on land. She dried her eyes in the tiny bathroom and stepped out into the quiet cabin. Everyone was outside, the laughter and music growing with each mile farther away from shore.

She heard a knock in a nearby room and hoped it was the captain. Maybe she could ask him if he could send her back on one of the zodiacs strapped to the back of the yacht. Plead seasickness, family emergency, anything to get out of here before she created any more regrets or humiliated herself by crying over Logan.

In the doorway to the small room where she'd heard the knock, she struggled to make sense of what she saw. Logan was going through documents in a box that she suspected had been locked before he'd got there.

"What are you doing?" she asked.

He snapped his head up, cracking it on the shiny wood cupboard that overhung the desk area. He cursed and clutched his skull.

"I said, what are you doing?" She stepped into the room.

Logan watched her for a moment, his face devoid of any emotion. "Close the door on your way out, please."

"Those aren't your papers."

"Trust me to keep us safe."

"Logan, you're scaring me."

"Trust me and leave."

"How can I trust you? I don't even know you." Her voice

was getting louder, and Logan placed a hand over her mouth, swinging the door shut with an eerie click.

She struggled against him. He was too calm, too strong, and it was freaking her out.

He was a thief. A liar. A snoop. He was not the man she thought she knew.

"Please, trust me. I won't hurt you," he whispered. His eyes met hers as he pleaded with her. He slowly lowered his hand, and she felt her eyes well up with tears of disappointment as she backed against the closed door, her heart thrumming madly in her chest.

"You lied to me."

"Ginger, please."

"You don't trust me like you said you did, and on top of it all, you're shutting me out. None of this is real and I was a fool to have forgotten, to have believed." She should be in a workshop right now, not trying to make a stupid happily ever after happen where it was obvious there would never be one.

"Ginger. Please."

"You know what I think of liars."

The door swung open, knocking her forward. It was Vito. Logan sat on the papers he'd been going through and pushed a hand through his hair.

"Sorry, Vito. The wife and I were having a fight."

Vito was on guard, obviously displeased with finding them in his office.

"How did you get in here? This room was locked."

There was a steeliness in Vito's voice that made Ginger shiver, and she found herself backing toward Logan. "It was open," she said. "I'm sorry."

Logan reached out, placing a comforting hand on her shoulder. She turned on him. "I'm still mad at you."

His gaze was pleading and she wasn't sure if it was about their fake fight, their real fight or something bigger than all of it.

Do whatever it is I ask you to without questioning it. Logan had asked that only an hour ago. *Promise you'll trust me.*

And she did trust him, just not with her heart. The man was a liar, and likely a thief to boot, and yet she still trusted him to keep her safe and was currently fighting an overwhelming instinct to protect *him*, keep *him* safe. It made no sense.

She was a sucker. It was likely that simple. But she could tell in a flash that whatever it was that Logan had been looking for, Vito didn't want him to find it. And as much as Ginger hated lies, she knew she had to get Vito out of the room in order to protect her husband.

She summoned tears, which wasn't too difficult, considering her level of disappointment. She sniffed once or twice. "He's been lying to me." She swiped at her eyes.

"Ginger..." Logan's voice held a warning.

"This room is off-limits," Vito snapped. "Private."

She brought more tears to the surface and threw her arms around their host, sobbing into his shoulder. "Please take me somewhere away from him. Please."

Vito hesitated and she continued crying, uncertain whether she could get the man off Logan's back.

He patted her shoulder at last and guided her out of the room. "My assistant will take care of you."

She nodded and sniffed. Moments later, Logan was at their side.

"I'll take her," he said gruffly.

"Can I go back to shore?" Ginger asked, pulling away from him. She didn't want Logan touching her, comforting her, whether for real or fake.

"Darling, lovers have spats," Vito said calmly. "I think you deserve a good time and a little pampering after the way he's treated you."

"I think she should go back," Logan said.

Ginger snapped a glare at him. He had no right to play-act the overprotective goon, and that's what his body language was saying loud and clear right now.

"Don't let him take this trip from you," Vito said softly, watching Logan. "You were looking forward to today. Have some girl time up on the sundeck. Let my staff pamper you, Ginger."

That did sound kind of good. "Then let's send Logan back."

Vito laughed, delighted by her reply. "Shall we send him to swim with the fishes?"

"With all that muscle? I doubt he'd be tasty," she retorted, allowing Vito to sweep her away to the upper deck where the party was going on. She didn't feel like joining in, but since she apparently seemed stuck aboard she may as well enjoy it. Or at least watch the resigned looking Logan from afar and see if she could figure out what his deal was and how she could divorce him in a way that wouldn't leave Annabelle all alone.

LOGAN HAD KNOWN GINGER WOULD head for the hills once she saw the real him. And how amateur was he to have let her walk in on him while he'd been recording documents for headquarters? It wasn't much, what he'd found. But compiled with everything else, it was enough to start closing in. And now, for the rest of the day, he'd have to keep an eye on her to ensure she didn't spill any beans or send suspicion his way.

But on a personal level, he knew he'd already lost her.

He was an idiot. He was smarter than to actually believe she'd truly fallen for a version of himself that was sustainable. And yet, like a fool, he'd still gone ahead and cared for her. Add in how she'd saved his butt by providing cover in that little office and he'd fallen even harder.

Now she was teetering around the deck with Vito's wife, Nadia, and Roxie, the wife of Greg, a jewelry designer. Ginger was wearing a bikini top and looked as tasty as the margarita she'd downed. That and vulnerable. Logan really wished she hadn't had a drink or two.

Out of the corner of his eye, he saw one of Vito's staff show something to Ted on the sly. A large diamond, Logan would assume, based on the man's reaction.

Vito and Ted laughed over something and headed down below. Vito nodded to Logan and Greg as he passed, inviting them to join in.

"We all want more profit, right?" Vito said as he herded them all into a private area just below deck. The stateroom was deceptively expansive, even for a yacht, with large, low couches laid out in a circle.

"Sure do," Ted agreed.

Logan took a seat in his hidden camera's one blind spot. He'd placed it just above a planter and it took in most of the room, with several microphones picking up sound.

"My dream is to take out those greedy middlemen," Vito said. "How much do you think they scrape off your profits?" he asked Ted.

The retailer frowned and shook his head. "A lot."

"It's an outrage! I own a mine in Africa and we produce some of the most flawless diamonds in the world. Why shouldn't I earn more on every stone? Why shouldn't you?" He scooted forward, dumping a small bag of cut gems into a tray on the coffee table in front of him.

Ted gasped, as did Greg, who then leaned back, rubbing a hand uncertainly over his belly.

Logan acted impressed. The mine produced good diamonds, that he knew. But Vito sure as heck didn't own it.

"Check them out." Vito passed each man a stone and a jeweler's eyepiece.

Logan swapped the eyepiece for his own, which had a camera inside. He inspected the stone, finding its origins untraceable. He couldn't confirm whether this stone was from the restricted shipment he'd been sent to apprehend.

"You cut them yourself?" he asked.

"That's been a problem for me so far. I'm hoping Greg could take that over."

Greg shrugged. "I can set them, but I don't know a lot about cutting them."

"I know a guy who might be looking for that kind of work," Logan said casually, pretending to still study the jewel. He could hear Ginger laughing out on the deck and he forced himself not to look out the room's upper windows that would give him a view of the sunny deck area's foot traffic.

"Is he reliable?" Vito asked.

Logan understood the code. Would the man rat them out?

"I'd put my life in his hands and not sweat it," he answered, looking up and passing the diamond back.

Vito watched him for a moment. "I'd like to meet him then. See a sample of his work, too, of course."

"Of course. When?"

"Tomorrow. I can't afford to keep sitting on my inventory. I have costs to cover."

Problem. Logan didn't know a guy. However, he could probably round up follow agent Zach to play the part. He'd have to come out of cover to contact him, but that wasn't much of an issue, seeing as he'd soon need to in order to bring in some manpower to set the trap and subsequent arrest, if Vito was as eager to make a move as it seemed.

"I can do tomorrow," Logan said. He'd figure something out. He wished Ginger could be further out of the picture so he could set things up, though, have her somewhere safe. But he'd make do. He had before and would again.

"You're a good man, Logan." Vito poured each man a glass scotch as he walked about the room. "I envision us with our own production line, controlling the product from mine to finger." He held up his hand, which sported a ring encrusted with diamonds. "Imagine the profits, men."

Ted was practically drooling on his shoes.

Outside, Ginger laughed again and Logan looked up, unable to resist the pull.

"Does your new wife want more than you can offer?" Vito asked, pausing beside Logan.

"More than you know," he said with a sigh.

"Then let's fix that, shall we?"

Logan looked up with a slight smile, wishing it was that easy.

"I'm in. My fiancée wants a huge house with a pool." Ted was running his fingers through the diamonds on the tray.

"My wife wants more vacations than I can afford," Greg added.

"That's women for you," Vito said with a smooth smile. He had the men eating out of his hand. "I'm not sure if you're ready for this kind of volume."

"Whatever you want me to do, count me in." Ted was perched at the edge of his seat, smiling like he'd won the lottery, completely clueless that he was jumping into something illegal, providing a cover for a ruthless and deadly man.

The room was quiet for a moment.

"What do we need to do to make this mine-to-finger plan a reality?" Logan asked, pointing to the tray of stones. "These are very nice, by the way."

Despite the way things were progressing, he was still far from busting the man. He needed uncut diamonds so he could prove their dirty origin and put Vito behind bars. Because once a diamond was cut, it was difficult to prove a thing.

"Here's my proposal. I supply them," Vito said. "Your guy cuts them." He pointed to Logan. "Then you set them," he said to Greg, who nodded. "Then Logan acts as wholesaler and distribution to Ted and another chain."

"We don't need a wholesaler," Ted said. "Sorry, Logan, but I want your portion of the cut." He laughed like it was a joke, but Logan could tell he was serious.

"We need someone to handle shipping," Vito said, his expression stern. "We're talking big time. Lots of cash tied up in each shipment. We can't let just anyone handle our volume." He was clearly irritated by Ted, and Logan had a feeling things could get bad. Fast. "More than your five measly stores can sell."

"I can expand."

Vito scowled at Ted before turning to Logan. "You have some big stores in need of wares on your wholesale list?"

He nodded. Ted was frowning, and Logan could tell he didn't quite get it yet. For a math-lete he was focusing on the wrong numbers, and didn't see that Logan was actually a cleaner, giving the whole thing a more legit feel, since Ted wouldn't be able to afford or move the number of diamonds Vito planned on sending down the line.

"So it looks like we have our own independent line," Logan said, raising his glass.

"To breaking free," Ted said, raising his own for a toast, eyeing Logan.

The men clinked glasses.

"Do you have any uncut diamonds?" Logan asked. "My friend will want to know what he's dealing with."

Vito waved to a man, who brought out a bag. Logan looked them over with his camera eyepiece. Unrestricted channels. These weren't the diamonds Vito needed to move through a new distribution line.

"They're nice."

Ted was leaning back against the couch, no doubt trying to figure out how much he might profit from this new deal. Logan hoped he didn't go out and buy that McMansion with the pool anytime soon, because the money train he was counting on wasn't going to leave the station—Logan could personally guarantee it.

"Are there any from different sources he'll need to cut?" he asked, dumping the diamonds back in their bag.

Another bag was silently brought out, one of Vito's men subtly moving his sport jacket aside to show Logan his piece.

Message received.

And as Logan suspected, this bag contained samples of the true mother lode. Smuggled blood diamonds. Restricted from trade and worth a ton to Vito because he likely hadn't ever paid for them. But someone had. With their blood.

This bag was exactly what was needed to put the man behind bars. However, simply being in possession of them wasn't what Logan was after. He wanted to catch the thug selling them, making a deal. Take down all the men around Vito—Ted included, if need be—and clean up the current source of blood diamonds.

Logan used his eyepiece to take a few shots, then was careful to swap it with Vito's before handing it back when he was done studying the stones.

"What kind of profits are we talking about?" Ted asked. His cheeks were flushed from the drinks and, undoubtedly, the excitement.

"Count on a million per shipment. Several times a year."

Greg swore and fumbled his empty scotch glass. Ted let out a whoop.

"Wow." Logan sat back.

"I told you it's wise to cut out the middleman." Vito grinned.

"I'll say," Logan muttered. By his calculations Vito must have enough diamonds in his possession to put him away forever. Plus some.

"I want to start moving ASAP because my inventory isn't making me any money collecting dust."

Logan nodded. Sounded good to him. As soon as he tried to make a cash-for-diamonds exchange the cuffs could come out, his mission would be complete and he could figure out how to hang on to his wife. The woman who didn't want anything to do with him at the moment.

"I'll see if my friend can make it to town tonight," Logan said.

Vito smiled. "I like you, Logan. You know how to get a job moving." He turned to Ted, but said to the room at large, "Just don't ever cross me and we'll all get along fine."

It was a warning Ted waved off. "Trust me, I don't want to share this with anyone else."

Ted's greed was going to get him killed, and his flippant disregard would likely send Vito out for some collateral.

Which meant Logan needed to send Ginger home. Immediately. Vito wasn't above doing whatever was needed to ensure that his partners kept their end of a bargain, and Ted was playing it fast and loose. And he'd been hanging out with Logan, possibly painting him with the same brush just through association.

As they headed up into the bright sunshine, Logan noted that Vito's guards were now armed. It was subtle but noticeable. They had revealed their cards and were displaying the fact that they were serious about protecting their hand.

To Logan's right, Nadia and Roxie were laughing with Ginger.

So innocent. So unaware.

Ginger glanced his way and he felt the power of her gaze hit him in the gut. That and the hurt lingering in her eyes. He knew she'd known he was not the man he'd said he was, but she'd expected something better than what she'd found and her look said it all.

She excused herself as Ted tumbled onto the bench beside his fiancée. The man had loose lips and was a danger to himself as well as Nadia. Logan wanted to warn him, but knew all he could do was throw interference if the man started talking, started messing things up.

"I need to use the restroom," Ginger said, moving past Logan. She stumbled as the boat pitched and Logan caught her, inhaling her scent. Her eyes met his and that something that surged between them was still there, full force, unbroken. Her gaze slowly lowered and she pulled her hand away from his chest, where it had landed when she'd righted herself in his arms.

"I'm sorry," he whispered.

She turned her face away.

"Ginger..."

She started walking away, and he felt a burn in his chest as he realized that the only thing he had left was to be the man she hated so he could keep her safe.

GINGER COULD BARELY REMEMBER HER afternoon on the yacht. She had a sunburn and the sweet margaritas had given her a headache. Logan had come back to their shared cottage only to ensure she made it back okay and to try and convince her to leave for home.

The nerve.

Just because he was done with her didn't mean she had to give up her workshops.

She dropped onto the bed, rolling over when she caught the familiar scent of his aftershave.

It was over.

Her head throbbed, as did her heart.

What had he been doing in that room? She was certain he'd broken in, rifled through the files. The entire day had felt off from start to finish.

He'd lied to her, then shut her out. He wasn't who she'd thought he was.

Something had gone on down below when all the men had gathered together. Some sort of deal. She shivered, thinking of how Vito's assistants were actually armed guards.

Her cell phone rang beside her in the darkening room, and she found herself wishing it was Logan even though she'd spent the entire day pushing him away, despite the curious looks from Nadia.

It was her grandmother. Ginger answered the call.

"How is Indigo Bay?" Wanda asked, her voice full of cheer.

Ginger burst into tears.

"What's wrong?" Her grandmother's voice was loaded with alarm. "Are you all right?"

"I met a man."

"And?" Wanda knew she was swearing off men.

"He had an accent."

"Oh, dear."

"He was wonderful. Special. It felt so real."

"And?"

She burst into a fresh bout of tears.

"Oh, honey. You're usually so pragmatic about your breakups."

"I know."

"This time was different, wasn't it?"

Ginger nodded, unable to speak. It *had* been different. She'd been fooling herself in a lot of ways, but the heartache she felt was more severe than any other she'd experienced, and she'd been with Logan for only a few days.

How was that even possible?

The truth was she'd fallen in love with her husband of convenience, and yet she didn't even know who he was or if the man she'd fallen for was anything more than an illusion meant to draw her in.

Whatever it was, it wasn't like anything she'd ever felt with other men. The love that had walloped her was the kind that could decimate a person. The kind that made it impossible to stand on your own two feet and face the world afterward. The kind where nobody else could ever step into her heart again because it was owned by someone else.

And for her, that person was the irreplaceable, mysterious Logan Stone.

That horrible, wonderful man.

And they'd been together only four days.

"What is it you always say?" her grandmother murmured. "Better to know now rather than after you marry him."

Gingers tears stopped. "I married him," she said softly.

Her grandmother started laughing.

"It's not funny."

"The lengths you'll go for a discount." Wanda was referring to her store's purchase offer. "You know that was all a joke, right, honey? A little nudge?"

"What?"

"I would still give it to you, of course, but it wasn't meant to...well, cause you to marry a stranger."

Ginger wanted to hang up, go to sleep and wake up back in her old reality. The one where she didn't feel brokenhearted or laughed at, and all she had to deal with was an annoyingly persistent lonely feeling.

Someone knocked at her door and, grumbling to herself, Ginger went to peek through the curtains to see who it was, expecting it to be the busybody Lucille again. She'd stopped by earlier to, Ginger felt, sniff out whether an actually honeymoon was going on in the little cottage. She'd managed to shoo the woman away before she accidentally let something slip, and had been avoiding making it look like anyone was in the cottage ever since. Even now she avoided turning on a light, letting the moonlight guide her instead.

As she lifted a corner of the curtain to peek out she saw it wasn't Lucille. It was one of the creepy security guards from Vito's yacht. Who took armed guards on a day's sail? It was after nine and the man had dead-looking eyes. There was no way she was answering the door without Logan being here.

Not that he was ever coming back.

And what had gone on today on the boat? Something was up and she had a feeling Logan wasn't the only thief on board.

She shivered and continued talking to Wanda, who was trying to coax her into letting go of her pain and anger.

"He lied to me, Grandma," she said quietly, not wanting the man on the porch to hear that she was indeed inside.

"About what?"

"I don't know exactly." Her heart hurt too much for her to

think, and the guy at the door was now rattling the knob. He knocked again.

Ginger slipped into the bathroom, where Logan had found the gun—whose was it? Had it actually been his? She shivered, considering her options. The lights were off, doors locked—Logan had reminded her to do that. There was no reason for the man to think she was inside the cottage unless he could hear her chatting through the walls.

She lowered her voice, planning to continue hiding out. She'd probably just forgotten something on the boat today and he was returning it.

"Logan isn't the man I thought I'd married."

"It sounds like you're running scared again."

"I'm not scared. And there is no 'again.'"

"You marry a man in a few days, hon, you aren't going to know a lot about each other. Anyone would find that a bit scary. Does the good outweigh the bad?"

Ginger paused to think about it even though she already knew the answer.

"It doesn't matter. He's gone." He'd got what he'd come for and was done. Had shut her out. Was in the process of leaving her.

Outside, she heard Vito's man leave, his footfalls on the cottage's steps heavy.

"Ginger, don't take this the wrong way," Wanda said, "but you tend to tell yourself a story."

"What do you mean?"

"That you're an easily swayed woman."

"I'm a sucker, Grandma."

"You're smart. You outsmart yourself every time and make sure your relationships fail."

"No, I don't." Did she?

"You're perceptive, and what you see in a man is always his best. I admire that. Most people see the bad, but not you. If you saw good in that man—enough to marry him in a couple of days flat—then that man is a keeper, Ginger McGinty. A keeper."

"No, Grandma. He's like Kurt and all the others. He's already left me."

He'd let her walk away. A man who loved a woman didn't do that. She'd thought he was the kind to stay, but what did it matter? He'd used her for a visa as per their agreement, and she'd been foolish to let herself believe that he might want to join her life in Blueberry Springs, that she was worth more than a piece of paper.

"Did he leave you or did you leave him? Because I've seen you leave a lot of men."

"I haven't left a single one of them." She was *not* her father.

"You left Kurt before he could leave you."

"No, he didn't come to school with me."

"You asked him to go clear across the continent. He couldn't afford it. He had a family ranch that needed his help on long weekends."

"He had brothers, and a man who loves a woman would have moved," Ginger said weakly.

"So it was a test? And he failed?"

She remained silent. Her once just argument felt a bit flat and selfish. Unfair, too.

"You could have gone to a closer school, but you didn't. What does that say about you?"

"High school relationships never last, Grandma."

"You were afraid he was going to leave you so you left him. Face it."

Ginger sighed. Okay, maybe that was a tiny bit true. But high school relationships rarely lasted once kids got out in the real world, so what did it matter?

"You choose men you know will leave, simply to reinforce your beliefs. You create self-fulfilling prophecies for all of your relationships."

"I don't."

"You do. When was the last time you dated a man who wasn't due to leave the country within a few months?"

"Grandma..." Ginger racked her brain for an example. Surely there had to be at least one besides her high school sweetheart. "But..."

She was really attracted to accents. Unless she was actually attracted to those men for reasons her grandma was stating...

"Honey, if you married that man, he's a keeper. So get over yourself and go find him."

"I have a business to run in Blueberry Springs and he has commitments here."

"Excuses."

"Good ones!"

"You're married, Ginger. Now's the time to make it work. You think me and my Tony walked into an easy, strong commitment? We didn't. We had to work for it. And why do you think I offered you money to marry Matias? Because I'm wealthy and generous?" Her grandma didn't wait for an answer. "No, because I saw what you were doing. You were pulling away, creating the self-fulfilling prophecy about being left, when he was doing all he could to stay. The money was a nudge to try and help you get over yourself."

Wanda was forgetting the reality ending. "He left me. And he wanted me for my medical plan."

"Of course he left. You all but kicked him out. The man was quiet and you started to act like it was personal. And as for the medical plan? You're just reaching."

"He was the one withdrawing!"

"Because you were picking silly fights and working longer hours and acting like you didn't care about him."

"But he..." Shoot. She kind of had started to push him away, hadn't she? Just like today—she'd started pushing Logan away, closing off. But it hadn't been all her today. He'd woken up distant and then broken into Vito's office.

Anything I say or do is about me. *Not you.*

He'd said that with heartfelt honesty, but she'd taken it personally, made it about her.

But he'd been snooping through stuff he shouldn't have. Plus he'd started pushing her away, and she knew what that meant.

"Stop making excuses," her grandmother said gently. "If you want this man, go get him before it's too late."

"But he has a secret side he won't let me know about."

"Then find a way to get to know it." Wanda said goodbye and ended the call.

And how was Ginger supposed to do that when she had a day and a half left here and he'd already walked away?

⌒∾⌒

IT WAS THREE IN THE MORNING AND Logan had one of the men from Vito's yacht in a headlock hold, his arms under the man's armpits from behind, his hands pinned behind the other man's neck. Logan was comfortable. The man under him trying to breathe sand was not.

He'd been one of Vito's guards on the yacht that afternoon and had no business at this time of night hanging outside Ginger's cottage. He'd come by around nine, now again. Nobody visited with good intentions at 3:00 a.m. and Logan had a feeling the armed man wanted his wife as collateral to ensure Logan did his boss's bidding, knew this game they were playing was in fact hardball.

Logan had spent some of his evening watching the honeymoon cottage before gathering more intel from his hidden cameras, sneaking aboard Vito's yacht, where he found a large stash of conflict diamonds, and finally calling up HQ. The team had begun working to set up meetings, traps, and by this time tomorrow he expected Vito to be in custody.

Zach had already had his meeting with Vito, mere hours after the yacht trip, and was on board to play the stone cutter's part. Things were moving fast.

"What are you doing here?" Logan whispered harshly in his captive's ear.

The man under him struggled, but didn't say a word. Logan began pushing the guy's head down, knowing it was awkward, painful and soon to be suffocating.

"I've got all night," he said calmly.

Never let anger impact your ability to get what you want on a job. Be ruthless.

Definitely don't think about the fact that the man had been trying to get into his wife's cottage for unknown reasons.

Wife.

Logan let up his hold without thinking, and the guy took

advantage, rolling, a knife brushing Logan's side as muscle memory had him dodging, eluding the hit.

He wrestled with the man, sand flying through the air as they fought for dominance. Logan felt the dune's grit between his teeth and his eyes stung when the man tossed sand in his face. Logan swung out with a leg, knocking his opponent down. He grabbed him, silently placing himself on top, pinning the man once again. Even though their fight had been quiet, he glanced up to ensure they hadn't woken anyone. The last thing he needed was to cause alarm as he wrestled a man capable of murder just outside the honeymoon cottage, which now had a lamp flicking on inside.

Honeymoon.

He shook his head.

What had his world come to?

He was sitting on an armed henchman on a cold dune instead of being inside that cozy little haven wrapped up in a woman who saw inside his soul and still seemed to care for him.

Well, she had until she'd finally seen the man he truly was.

But she'd cared for him once. And maybe could again.

Logan cursed under his breath as the heartache ripped through him. The man under him opened his mouth to scream and Logan knocked him out with one punch before sliding off his limp form with a dejected sigh.

This wasn't the life he wanted.

GINGER HAD BEEN SLEEPING IN fits and starts.

What her grandmother had said on the phone had struck a chord.

She left men. They didn't leave her. Well, they finally took a walk, but it was because she pushed them away repeatedly until that was the only thing left that they could do.

A keeper. Logan was a keeper.

There had been plenty of good in Logan.

She didn't know him, that was true.

But she trusted him, even though he'd been up to things she didn't understand. How could she possibly still trust him?

She rolled out of bed and flicked on the bedside lamp. It was three in the morning and she thought she'd heard something on the front porch. At this time of night Logan was usually wandering the beach, and she wondered if he was returning. She moved to the window, to find the moon shining bright.

No Logan.

What did she expect? To see him rising out of the ocean like a marine again?

Like a marine.

The gun. The secrets.

She stood in the middle of the room, mulling things over. Then she began rifling through the small cottage, looking for clues. She started in the bathroom, searching for the mysterious gun. Behind the toilet tank, inside it, under the sink. When she came up empty-handed, she turned around in the small room.

Who was Logan Stone and why did she have a strong feeling things were hidden inside this cottage?

She moved to the bedroom. Under the mattress? No. Too obvious.

Hands on her hips, she stared at the wall beside the couch. A watercolor print of the beach. She strode over to it, lifting it from its place. She turned the picture around. Nothing was taped to its back, nothing on the wall.

She sighed and studied the room. Where would she hide something? She lifted the picture to rehang it and heard something slide, like it was tucked behind the papered back. She peeled away a corner of the backing. A passport was inside.

She hesitated, then opened it. There was a photo of Logan Stone, but the man's name wasn't Logan.

She continued her search, reminding herself to breathe as she eventually came up with a knife, some sort of gadget she didn't understand, a cell phone, cash and a gun.

If she didn't know any better, Logan Stone was either a spy or a man on the run.

But how did he end up with Annabelle if he was a spy?

Which meant he was a man on the run. Hiding.

From who?

He didn't like Vito. She could feel that coming off him.

But Vito didn't seem to mind Logan.

There was something there. She could feel it.

Someone banged on the front door and Ginger squeaked.

The lights were on. She was obviously awake, which meant there was no hiding out this time.

"Ginger! It's Ted. Is Nadia with you?"

Ginger went to the door. Ted was looking pale and worried.

"I can't find her anywhere."

"What do you mean?"

He held up a note. "She said she was going for a walk. But when I got back from the bar where I was talking with Vito I couldn't find her. Nobody's seen her for hours and the police say they won't start looking until she's been gone twenty-four hours or there's evidence of foul play."

"It's..." Ginger checked the time ",,,three thirty in the morning."

"I've looked everywhere." He dropped onto the couch, his hands in his hair. "I don't know what to do. Who to ask."

Logan.

I care for you. A lot.

Anything I say or do is about me. *Not you.*

Whatever happens today, just trust me. Know that you know the real me.

But she didn't know the real him. She knew that because she had a passport with a name in it that wasn't the one on their marriage certificate.

He'd known something was up today. He hadn't been nervous about sailing, he'd been nervous about Vito. That made Ginger worry that Nadia was in trouble. And Logan was the man who knew what to do about it.

But how was she going to find him?

LOGAN HAD TIED UP VITO'S henchman and left him in the scuba shed, knowing the man would be discovered shortly after dawn if Logan didn't hurry up and deal with the loose ends that were starting to unravel.

He hurried to the Tiki Hut, popping the lock meant to

keep trespassers at bay, and removing a panel behind the bar that he'd added months ago. Behind the false front was a stash of gadgets, and he set himself up in the quiet to begin running through his feeds once again, looking for new intel, peeking out every once in a while to make sure he wasn't being scouted.

Vito's yacht had moved a few hours ago and was now anchored just offshore. Logan guessed a delivery of diamonds was going to occur, although that didn't quite feel right. However, Vito had arranged to meet with Ted, Greg, Logan and Zach aboard the boat again just after dawn. Maybe he was stockpiling diamonds and was ready to move even faster than Logan had anticipated.

Logan's main camera on the yacht had been knocked askew, so he could tell people were aboard via its audio but could see nothing as its lens was now aimed at the ceiling. In other words, nothing much definitive in the way of intel.

He pinged Zach Forrester, who relayed that the team was on the move and ready for an early morning rendezvous, and that Logan was to stay put until given the word.

Logan debated catching some shut-eye, but instead flipped his feed over to the recording from the cottage. He'd set up the surveillance like always, as he did when he settled anywhere. He knew Ginger was likely safe, with her main threat tied up in the shed, but he wanted to ensure no further dangers had appeared on her horizon.

He paused before hitting the button that would invade her privacy, then braced himself as he watched her cry into her phone in a scene recorded a few hours earlier. She peeked out the curtains around the time Mr. Henchman had popped by for his first visit. Logan had been in the tall grass near the cottage, watching, waiting, knowing the chances of something happening were pretty great. He'd also managed to successfully avoid Paul around that time. The police officer knew the reason for Logan's impromptu wedding and didn't seem to care that his current stay was legal. Paul was waiting for him to screw up, for there to be a lapse in his paperwork so he could send Logan back home. But there wouldn't be a lapse.

But Ginger. Why was she was crying?

Obviously because of him.

He'd lied and she hated liars. He'd asked her to trust him, asked her to not take anything he did personally, had assured her the best he could, and he'd failed. He could have told her the truth, pulled out of the agency, and seeing her cry made him wonder why he hadn't done that.

Right. That didn't get the job done. Didn't save villages from killers like Vito.

Logan fast-forwarded through hours of Ginger tossing and turning in bed, her supple form glowing in the strip of moonlight that slipped through the curtains. He paused the feed as it zipped past three o'clock—almost an hour ago. He rewound to the time when Vito's man had shown up for his second visit.

She'd woken up and turned on a light. Looked out the window. Then she'd proceeded to rip the place apart while he took care of Vito's man out in the sand dunes.

Logan rubbed a knuckle across his forehead, cringing as he watched her find his passport.

He stood, cursing. Then, realizing he was supposed to be hiding, he sat again.

Worst agent in the world. That's what he became when she was around.

He watched, curious as to what else she'd find, and what her grainy black-and-white reaction would be.

She discovered weapons, cash. Just about everything, and he found himself smiling. She might act like she was just a bubbly, happy, small-town gal, but she had a lot going on. A lot he liked. Still smiling, he wondered if she'd consider becoming an agent.

He was almost caught up to real time with the recorded feed when he saw Ginger go to the door.

No!

Logan almost stood up again, ready to dash across the sand.

Had Vito sent a follow-up man?

What if Logan had already lost her?

He sped up the recording, his breath coming in jagged bursts. He nearly died of relief when he saw it was only Ted who'd come by, without his fiancée.

The man showed Ginger a note and Logan knew—Nadia was missing.

Ginger turned and looked straight into the hidden camera, and Logan knew it was time to tell her everything.

CHAPTER 6

Ginger went to the door, not at all surprised to find Logan standing there, decked out in black clothing. "Nadia is missing."

"I know," he said, setting her skin on fire as he brushed past her. His eyes swept the room, picking up Ted's slumped form on the couch, the weapon and passport she'd unearthed and not put away.

"We need to talk," she said.

"I know."

"Privately."

"Agreed."

They both turned, marching to the bathroom as if of one mind.

Logan closed the door behind them and Ginger leaned against the vanity, arms crossed over her red pajamas.

"I'm sorry I had to lie to you."

Ginger had been ready to drill him with questions, but paused as he took her hand, his expression softening with hope when he saw his rings still on her finger. "I need you, Ginger."

"No, you don't."

"I do. You make me feel real, alive. You're part of the life I want."

"You lied to me."

"Yes."

"Because you're a..." Which scenario should she pop on him? "...a thief."

"A thief?" He hesitated as though about to agree, then shook his head.

Yeah, she didn't quite believe that one, either. Even though he had stolen her heart.

"You're a man on the run. You cross borders with various passports and—and..." She was too tired to think. "...you're involved with something unbelievable, something out of the movies."

"Close."

"You're an undercover cop?" she asked hopefully. She kind of liked that one. It wasn't too scary. "A spy?"

He brushed her cheek with the backs of his knuckles. "Just know that I'll do whatever I can to keep you safe, and any time I don't tell you the truth it's because I'm protecting you."

She was so ready to cave. But she needed to stand strong. They couldn't have a true relationship with secrets.

"Nice cover. Does that work on all your wives?"

"You're the only one."

She looked down at their linked hands, not remembering when that had happened.

She'd chosen Logan, certain he would leave her. She hadn't given Kurt a truly fair shake all those years ago, and, as Wanda had pointed out, she consistently went for men who left her. Were destined to and made no bones about that being their intention.

Then she blamed them for it.

"Logan?"

"Yes?"

"Please tell me the truth—is what's between us real?"

"Yes."

She watched him for a long moment. His eyes were a soft gray—the color they became when he was the man she knew, loved and understood. What he said was true. He believed they had something, too.

The problem was, she didn't know how long he'd last before the other guy with the slate-gray eyes would take over, acting edgy and distant. The man she'd seen on Vito's boat. The man who'd escorted her back to the honeymoon cottage and told her to lock the doors if she wouldn't go home to Blueberry Springs.

"Who's Vito?"

"He's not a good person," Logan said hesitantly. There was a story there, that was for certain.

"I know that. And you don't like him. Why?"

"He's not a good person," Logan repeated with a sigh. "I really need you somewhere safer than Indigo Bay right now."

Her mind flicked to Vito's man who'd come by that evening. She had a bad feeling about him, and wasn't sure why, but had a suspicion he was connected to Nadia's disappearance.

"Did Vito take Nadia?"

Logan's eyes shifted ever so slightly, revealing his surprise, as well as the truth.

Ginger crossed her arms. "So how are we getting her back?"

"Wait. I thought we were having a moment and figuring out our relationship."

"We were and we did. I trust you, forgive you, and know we have a ton of work left to do on our relationship. But Nadia is missing."

He nodded, his brow wrinkled in confusion, even though an amused smile was playing at his lips. "So you and I, are we...?"

"About to kiss and make up?" She leaned closer, wondering if she was being incredibly hopeful, or stupid in trusting him and believing that something between them might last. "Yes."

She kissed him long and slow.

"And now we go save my friend."

LOGAN COULDN'T QUITE BELIEVE IT.

Ginger might have just forgiven him. At least a little bit. Either that or she was simply using him to help her find Nadia.

But that kiss? It had been an I-forgive-you kiss. One that held promises of later.

There had been no big fight. No big declarations of love or misguided trust or any of that. Just a "who are you and I forgive you let's go save the world and talk about our marriage later."

That worked for him, but it also confused him worse than a Rubik's Cube. He didn't know where he stood, didn't know how much she knew or understood, only that they needed time. Lots of time.

He saw his reflection in the bathroom mirror, his confusion and uncertainty apparent.

He currently had no orders to move forward, but a missing person connected to the case meant a call-in. "Can you excuse me a moment?"

Ginger left the bathroom and he locked himself in as he contacted HQ, letting them know Nadia was missing. They already knew that. She was on the yacht and so was Greg's wife, Roxie.

Collateral.

And that was why Vito's man had kept coming around Ginger's cottage. Thank goodness she hadn't opened the door or she'd be tied up on that yacht, too.

The very idea of her being that close to danger made Logan want to slam his fist through the bathroom door.

He needed to get her out of here, find a safe place for her, as the team was going to perform a takedown at this morning's meeting with Vito, assuming he revealed enough details that they could slap a binding conviction on him. If nothing else, they had him on kidnapping and possession of what amounted to a crap ton of stolen, restricted diamonds. That would put a kink in his business plans for a decade or two. But Logan needed Ginger far away in case things went haywire.

As he opened the bathroom door he caught sight of Ted silently freaking out on the couch. He'd rather leave the man as much in the dark as possible so he didn't mess things up, but Ginger needed to know enough that she could leave town with Annabelle and act like the smart woman Logan knew she was.

"Ginger?" He called her into the bathroom again, closing the door behind them.

"Are you okay?" She looked worried.

"I can't tell you who I am, but know that I'm a man who has sworn to keep you safe."

"You'll never be able to tell me, will you?"

He realized that his secret identity would always stand between them, always be a problem for Ginger.

"Not today. And right now I need you to take Annabelle out of town until I come get you."

"Why?"

"It's probably best you don't ask me any questions I might have to lie about, but know that it's for your safety as well as hers. I'm counting on you to help me."

She slowly nodded, heaving a big sigh. For a moment he thought she was going to walk, judging by the fear and uncertainty flickering over her features. But then she looked up, her expression one of resolve. "Okay."

"You trust me to keep you safe?"

"Always."

He gave her a kiss—a brief one, as there was no time for distractions.

He let them out of the bathroom and swept up the various gadgets Ginger had found, tucking them onto his body. It felt familiar, though not like the man he wanted to be when around Ginger. But he'd worry about that later.

Right now he had a job to do, and one of them was ensuring his wife remained safe.

GINGER WASN'T SURE HOW TO HANDLE her new reality. She was sitting in her little rented convertible with the top up, Logan standing beside her, leaning in to give her a quick rundown on how to tell if she was being tailed, how to shake someone, what to do if someone tried to rear-end her or run her off the road.

She grabbed his hand. "I can't do this."

The sun was starting to creep over the horizon, her friend was missing, Ginger had to take a girl to a safe house, and she was fairly certain her husband was a spy.

A spy!

She'd *married* a spy. Who on earth married a spy?

She was legally married to a man with guns strapped to his side and totally owning it.

And why had he needed a visa if he was a spy? Was she some sort of cover for him? Did that nullify their marriage?

Oddly, she wasn't sure how she felt about that since coming to terms with the fact that she quite liked the guy and wanted to spend some time with him. Lots of time.

But Annabelle. The girl couldn't be part of an elaborate cover, could she?

Man, was Ginger ever confused.

And by the sound of things, her time on Vito's yacht had actually been set up as some sort of meeting that had gained Logan the intel he needed to go in today to arrest the man. She didn't want to even think what Logan planned to arrest him for, seeing as kidnapping Nadia and Roxie seemed to be only the icing on the cake and not the full meal.

Logan, his eyes intense, crouched beside her. "It's going to be okay."

"No. No, it's not."

"It is. This is my job."

"No, it's not." She didn't know what was wrong with her, only that she was ready to cry, ready to crumble.

"Ginger, look at me."

Her eyes had been locked on the long knife strapped to his calf and she glanced up, meeting those gray eyes, so steady, so sure.

"This is who I am."

"No, it's not."

"It is."

"No! You're kind and caring and not a killer."

"Ginger..."

She was crying, at a loss over how a guy so sweet and tender could also be a man with weapons strapped to him, ready to swing in and save the day by any means required.

"Please be him for me," she begged, sliding out of the car. She loved the soft side of Logan and didn't know what to do with this spy side. He was deadly, dangerous. About to walk into something that could end his life.

"I have a job to do. People to save."

She placed her hands on either side of his face. "Then do it, and come back to me and be the man I fell in love with."

He crushed her in a sudden hug, his breathing jagged. "I want to be married to you, Ginger. I want a real life."

"Then we'll find a way, because I'm not leaving you. You're my husband and you're a keeper. Please, come back to me."

"I swear I will. I swear."

And when they kissed, she tasted the union of their salty tears.

LOGAN STRODE INTO THE MARINA for his meeting with Vito. The agency had eyes on Ginger, and said she'd collected Annabelle and left town, heading toward Charleston. But that's where their tail ended, because it was needed on the docks. Logan had placed a tracer on her car, made sure her cell phone was charged and done all he could to keep her safe with such short notice.

His Ginger. His wife.

She loved him. Wanted to be with him.

Darned if that didn't make this the happiest day of his life. He whistled as he moved among the docks, the boats rocking gently, their cables every so often clanging jauntily against their masts. He was wearing a wire, and the marina was stacked with agents acting as early morning workers.

Vito was going down today.

Logan would battle the bad guy, save Nadia and Roxie, then go home—to Ginger—and figure out how to be a husband.

And all before the sun was fully up and the world awake.

Mission complete.

Easy.

He turned down the last dock, closing in on Vito's boat.

He was hit by a shock wave as the boat exploded, the force slamming the wind from his lungs as he flew through the air, hitting the water hard before its icy, salty chill swallowed him whole.

CHAPTER 7

Logan tested his limbs as he coughed the water from his lungs. After his cold, brutal dunking in the sea, he'd somehow managed to pull himself back up on the dock, woozy from the shock and still fighting not to lose consciousness. He hoped his wire was waterproof.

He rolled onto his back, catching sight of a gutted, burning hull. Vito's yacht. Well, he supposed a working wire was the least of his worries.

Diamonds, uncut, littered the dock as Logan twisted onto his side. There went months of undercover work.

Although, then again, maybe not completely. Agents were already swarming the area, retrieving bodies from the water, one quickly collecting the diamonds.

Logan watched Vito be pulled from the water. Then Nadia and Roxie, too. They'd all be okay. Both women's eyes were opening as they struggled to come back around after their unexpected dip into the frigid ocean.

He eased back onto his back, wheezing as he tried to bolster himself into moving into a more upright position. "I'm too old for this crap," he said as Zach Forrester came up alongside him.

His friend offered him a hand, pulling him up, then giving him a shoulder to lean on while acting as though he was reading Logan his rights so he could arrest him. All part of maintaining his cover and protecting agents.

"Is it just the pain talking?" Logan asked. "Because right now I want out."

He knew it wasn't just his aching muscles making him say that.

Zach nodded. "Probably." He gave him another assessing glance. "But you really are out, aren't you?"

Logan waved to the smoking remains of the several-million-dollar yacht, trying to distract himself from the images of Ginger that floated through his mind. "Why blow up the boat? That takes all the fun out of the takedown."

"You're lucky you weren't on board."

Logan's knees seemed to lose their ability to lock.

"Whoa there." Zach braced him with a hand on his chest. He glanced around to check if anyone was watching. "Want to sit?"

"I'm good."

His fellow agent studied him for a moment. "Aw, man."

"What?" Logan looked around for the source of his friend's disappointment. All he could see was billowing smoke, diamonds, scurrying agents and a whole lot of handcuffs. Enough to warrant the look, but he knew it wasn't the cause.

"You're in love, aren't you?"

Logan snorted but smiled. He was.

"And my guess is you want to tell her who you really are so you can have an honest relationship."

Logan sighed. He did.

"When you fall in love," Zach continued, "things change, such as your priorities and where you place your attention."

Logan rubbed his jaw, unable to argue that point.

"The Logan I knew a few months ago would have sensed that double-crosser's explosion coming before anyone else."

"Double-crosser?"

"Yeah, the guy who delivered a new stash of diamonds a few hours back. They were all hanging out, like everything was cool, until literally a minute ago. We heard him over the ears you set up. He announced he wanted more money. Vito said no. The guy left, then boom." Zach raised his hands in the air. "We were listening in, letting it play out, and did not see that explosion coming." He clapped Logan on the shoulder. It hurt. "You're a lucky man, you know that?"

He agreed. He was definitely lucky.

Zach spun him around and slapped cuffs on him. Logan pretended to be indignant, shaking his head at the supposed injustice of it all. He added for any audience, "It wasn't me! I just forgot something on Vito's boat yesterday. I swear!"

"You've become a danger to yourself," Zach said quietly.

Logan looked at him in confusion as he led him toward the collection of police cars in the marina parking lot. His fellow agent opened his mouth to speak, then shook his head. He said lightly, "Dude, do you even hear the fire department's sirens going off around us right now?"

Logan frowned. "Must have hit the water harder than I thought." He tilted his head to the side as though draining water from his ear canals.

"Well. Anyway, I'm opening a private security business. You're welcome to join me if you'd like."

"You fall in love?"

"Nope." He grinned. "But I know an agent can punch his card only so many times." They walked in silence for a moment, the dock feeling unsteady under Logan's feet. "Come join me."

Logan barely hesitated before agreeing, wishing he wasn't cuffed so he could shake Zach's hand. He didn't know what he was doing, only that he was listening to that little voice inside him that started up whenever Ginger was around.

He thought it might be the voice of hope.

Zach pushed Logan into a waiting police car to maintain his cover. Paul was behind the wheel, grinning at his catch. Until he saw that Logan was soaking wet and would leave his squad car drenched.

But little did the triumphant Paul know, Logan wasn't truly being arrested or processed, and he'd be released later in the day under the umbrella of "wrong place, wrong time." That ought to drive the poor, well-meaning officer nuts.

"By the way, who gets married while undercover?" Zach muttered under his breath as he started to close the car door.

"A lucky man, Zach. A very lucky man."

GINGER HAD RECEIVED WORD THAT IT was okay to return to Indigo Bay. Nadia and Roxie had been rescued and were at the hospital receiving non-urgent care. Logan was fine and would see her in Indigo Bay.

She bought Annabelle a sandwich that served as brunch and herself a coffee before hitting the road, enjoying the palm trees lining the way, the ocean lapping to the east. She helped pass the time by making the girl laugh with her silly jokes as they headed back to the little ocean town that had been Ginger's home for the past week, as well as the location of her honeymoon.

Honeymoon.

Some deal that was. She wanted to have a real one. One where they consummated their union and said sweet things like "I love you."

Assuming that was true.

To distract herself from the uncertainty that kept creeping in, Ginger told Annabelle stories about Blueberry Springs, the bears, the mountains, the hiking. The girl was enthralled and her enthusiasm and questions made Ginger long for home.

Home.

What were she and Logan going to do? A long distance marriage would be doomed from the word *go* and she wanted to give their relationship a real try, with neither of them leaving or pushing the other away, or holding anything back. But if Logan was indeed a spy, there were always going to be things he couldn't tell her.

Was she okay with that? Could she still let love in, without fears interfering if she didn't know his entire story?

She pulled up outside the honeymoon cottage, where she'd been told to go. She hadn't been sure if she was supposed to drop Annabelle off first, so she'd brought her along. It seemed riding in the car made the girl sleepy and she was dozing again. Or maybe it was simply due to their early morning start.

Logan was waiting on the step and he stood as she put the car in Park. She relaxed, knowing he was truly okay.

She watched him come closer, and seeing him move made

her whole body awaken. She loved that man. She didn't have a clue who he really was, only that there was something about him, some part of him that had hooked her.

She would leave Blueberry Springs for a man like him—if he was indeed the real deal that she'd seen and fallen for.

She rolled down the window, not wanting to wake Annabelle by opening or closing the door.

Logan wasn't wearing black any longer. He was in jeans and a T-shirt, and looking more relaxed and at ease than she'd ever seen him.

He bent down to hold the frame of the window. "So, I quit."

"What?"

"I'm no longer an agent for a transnational agency that ensures the safety of others."

"What exactly is that again?" Special police? FBI? CIA? Military? So many options.

"Most people call me a spy."

"I knew it." She stared through the windshield, not really seeing the pink cottage in front of her.

"No, you didn't."

"I did."

"Okay, you did." He grinned.

"So that explains the secrets? The lies?"

"It's what we spies do."

She supposed that was true. But that still left the question of how much of the man she knew was a cover and how much was real.

"Are you really Australian?"

"Right-o, mate. Born and raised. Joined the army after my

first marriage didn't work out. Sold the cattle station. Parents are gone."

She'd married a spy from Australia.

And he cared for her. That part was real, right?

"Why did you quit the agency, Logan?"

"Because I love you and I know it's difficult being married to a spy."

Loved her. That felt good.

But could you really just quit being a spy?

And had he really quit for her?

If so, that was really romantic.

"And so now we're going to act married?" she asked, thinking out loud, trying to envision this sudden new life. "Live together? Do the whole marriage thing for real?"

"If you have room in your life for a man like me."

Of course she did.

"But how is that going to work?" She glanced at Annabelle, who was now awake. "Are we staying here in Indigo Bay?"

"I have a room with stripes," Annabelle said.

"I heard," Ginger said softly. The only way for her to give something a try with Logan would be to stay here and give up her shop. Maybe her grandmother wouldn't mind running it for a bit so she could stick around and feel things out.

"You know Ginger lives in the mountains," Logan said, speaking to Annabelle.

"Do you ski?" the girl asked.

"Sometimes," Ginger admitted.

"Do you live in Australia?" Annabelle's next question was laced with suspicion.

"No."

"Do you have stripes on your flag?"

Logan answered for her. "Yes, Annabelle. What do you say? Want to go check out the mountains? Maybe spend a week there?"

The young woman's eyes lit up and Ginger's heart lifted.

"Yes, please!"

"What do you think, Ginger? Could we spend a week in Blueberry Springs and see which place suits us all best? We could explore whether you and I are a match worth pursuing, too."

His face was close to hers, his eyes so soft and kind. This was the man she knew, the one she'd fallen for. The man she'd follow anywhere—the real one under the spy persona. The spy persona that had struggled and succeeded in keeping her safe. The spy persona that had been laid to rest.

"Logan Stone, or whoever you are, I happen to know we're a very sweet match and that you might just end up staying in Blueberry Springs for longer than a week."

EPILOGUE

Logan had spent a fun week in Blueberry Springs with Annabelle and his wife. The small mountain town was lively and quaint, its citizens friendly, nosy and very curious about him. It wasn't the kind of place where a guy could lie low, that was for sure. Not that there was much need for that now that Vito and his men were in jail and Logan had officially retired from the agency.

And Annabelle loved it. She was ready to move in, and had her eye on a job at a little cafe called Wrap It Up. She loved the brownies there and was already angling to get Mandy, the owner, to hire her.

It was all perfect except when it came to crime—Logan's main skill set when it came to an occupation. The problem was that crime didn't stand a chance with all the busybodies wandering around, minding everyone's business. They reminded him of the lady who ran Sweet Caroline's back in Indigo Bay. Well-meaning, but wow. A tad over the top, and making his security skills somewhat redundant. What was he going to do for a living in this place?

Zach had thought Logan could offer some basic home security packages, but Logan figured he'd likely get more business setting up puppy cams. Cameras where owners could peek in on their dog to see how it was doing while they were at work.

That would certainly be better than nothing, since the busybodies currently had the market cornered on protecting their own, nudging out a need for his professional services. Right now, in fact, they were protecting his wife, not letting him into the church where his own wedding was scheduled to take place—this time with his legal name on the certificate even though he'd taken the cover name Logan as his own as it seemed like everyone he cared about called him that anyway.

The issue was a little old woman with a cane who was barricading him from entering. His friends—all of them agents—were waiting on the groom's side of the aisle within, and would be laughing their butts off if they knew what he'd come up against.

"I'm Logan. I don't believe we've met."

"How do we know you're who you say you are?" the woman asked him, arms crossed.

"Do I need to sneak in a window?" he asked. The church was right there, all grand and beautiful on the gorgeous spring day.

Annabelle was already inside, having spent the morning racing around the small town, oohing and ahhing over the tall peaks that guarded Blueberry Springs. It turned out she loved hiking.

"I'm marrying Ginger."

"Wrong!" declared the woman. "She's already married. Now, move along or we'll call in Scott."

He was tempted to lift the woman, place her to the side, then skip up the steps to meet his destiny. But he knew small towns. It was best to play nice.

"Who's Scott?"

"The town's police officer."

Just one police officer? That sounded hopeful. Logan would bet there were times when the man could use some backup, and maybe a little added surveillance from a contractor such as himself.

The woman took out a flask, knocking back a sip.

"What have you got there?" Logan asked.

"Sherry."

"Good choice."

She considered him, then passed him the flask so he could take swig. "I know who you are. I'm just giving you a hard time." She held out her hand to shake his. "The name's Gran."

"Gran?"

"It's what everyone calls me, and since you'll be making this place home I suppose you'll need to know that. By the way, my granddaughter runs an outreach program from the hospital's continuing care area. Your girl might get a lot out of it and give you a little more time with your new wife. Plus she'd have more of the independence she obviously loves."

"You've met her?" Logan was surprised. He knew a few of Ginger's friends had shown AnnaBee around town, taking her in like she was one of their own. It had made both of them love the town all the more.

"She's a real sweetheart. She did crafts with us at the home yesterday. She has a thing for stripes, doesn't she?"

"She does."

"You have good intentions with our Ginger?" Gran asked, the question not so much pointed as curious. He could tell she'd already made up her mind about him and that it was all okay. She was just giving him the gears so he knew Ginger had a town that would side with her if he ever stepped out of line.

Not that he planned to. When you finally found the right woman, you cherished her, loved her and did everything you could to keep her happy.

"I promise to be good," he replied.

"That's not the first time I've heard you make that promise," said a playful voice. Ginger came up beside him, dressed for the wedding. In her sleek, gorgeous gown she looked even more amazing than in her green dress from Indigo Bay, and because they were sort of already married, he didn't consider seeing her in her wedding dress as bad luck. Because she was his talisman.

And she was his.

He was one lucky man.

She reached up to give him one of those kisses that knocked his world off its orbit, then asked, "Were you waiting long?"

The question took him back to the moment they'd met while trying to fib their way into the resort's couples party. The moment he'd become a goner and his whole world had changed for the better.

"I'd wait till the end of the world for you, Ginger. The end of the world."

GINGER SIGHED HAPPILY FROM HER spot at the head table. A real wedding. For her and Logan, her husband, the love of her life. Across the room he was chatting with his friends. They had to be agents. They all sat with their backs to the wall, their expressions somber, sport jackets tucked and buttoned as though hiding weapons, instead of draped over chair backs like many of the other male guests' were, as the hall's temperature increased during the evening.

Sure, she wasn't certain when her husband's birthday was, but when you found the right person, you just knew, and that was it. Mates for life, as he'd said in his vows.

Things happened in threes for Ginger. They also happened for a reason, and all those good things, like her grandmother had always promised.

At long last.

"Glad you came to your senses," Wanda said, joining her.

"You were right. Thanks for putting my head on straight about me and men."

"I meant with the dress. I like the longer train."

Ginger smiled at her grandma, knowing that wasn't what she'd meant. She leaned over and gave her a hug.

She would have lost out on a lot if she'd left Logan. The past few weeks in Blueberry Springs had been incredible. He and Annabelle had stayed at a B and B, since Ginger was basically living in a glorified storeroom. She and Logan had had a few late night "dates" that had been wonderful, and she hoped they'd soon settle into their new lives and she could have him a little more often. But the way they'd been going about things had worked okay, too. Slow, steady. Nothing to freak either of them out.

"I heard you paired up a few people during your week away," her grandmother said. "I hope you gave them the store's business card," she added with a wink.

"Of course." Ginger glanced around the room. "But a little closer to home I can think of a few people who could also use a little push in that direction." She waved to her friend Devon Mattson, who she'd gone to university with and was now running for mayor.

"Devon," she called, "I heard Olivia Carrington is developing a new cosmetics line."

His expression hardened. He and Ginger's roommate, Olivia, had had it big during their university days. Big love followed by a big fight. And they were both still single a decade later. That could hardly be a coincidence.

"Did you know the flowers in the meadow that Jill is using for her creams would be a perfect match for what Olivia needs? It might just help your campaign, too." So far, the old mayor had a definite lead, what with Devon's devil-may-care demeanor inhibiting his campaign. She hoped he'd win—not just because of the way he talked about small business tax reform for the town, but because he would be good at it.

"I'm not desperate enough to dig up the past," Devon grumbled, and Wanda gave Ginger a knowing look.

Devon's expression turned mischievous. "Oh, and congratulations. When's the baby due?"

"Don't you dare start that rumor!" Ginger laughed, knowing that a lot of people in the small town suspected that their hasty marriage was actually a shotgun wedding. They would surely be confused when she and Logan celebrated their first wedding anniversary weeks before anyone expected.

Logan rejoined her and her grandmother, giving Ginger a long, sweet kiss.

"Not a bad rumor," he murmured, kissing her again as Devon slipped away.

"Yeah?"

"Yeah. I hear you want ten rug rats."

"I thought that was you? And anyway, don't believe everything you hear." She lightly placed a finger against Logan's lips.

"Are you really going to set Devon up with someone?" Wanda asked.

"I am," Ginger said with a nod. It was time he either buried the hatchet with Olivia or moved on.

"Good luck with that," her grandmother muttered.

"Challenge accepted."

"I have complete faith in Ginger," Logan said, kissing her temple. "She sees things others don't. And I don't know what the world would do without my sweet matchmaker."

∞

What comes next? Try the next Indigo Bay Sweet Romance Series book, Sweet Sunrise, by Kay Correll. Or think you missed others in the series? Here's the full list...

Indigo Bay
Sweet Romance Series

Six fun beach reads by Six fabulous authors

Sweet Dreams (Book 1) by Stacy Claflin
Sweet Matchmaker (Book 2) by Jean Oram
Sweet Sunrise (Book 3) by Kay Correll
Sweet Illusions (Book 4) by Jeanette Lewis
Sweet Regrets (Book 5) by Jennifer Peel
Sweet Rendezvous (Book 6) by Danielle Stewart

Want to check out Ginger's hometown of Blueberry Springs and see where Logan and Ginger ended up? Dive on it! The Veils and Vows series is an irresistible new series by Jean Oram where you can catch up with all your good friends! Turn the page for the latest and greatest from *New York Times* bestselling romance author Jean Oram.

VEILS & VOWS

AN IRRESISTIBLY FUN NEW SERIES BY

JEAN ORAM

NEW YORK TIMES BESTSELLING AUTHOR

WWW.JEANORAM.COM

READ, DREAM, LAUGH & LOVE

The latest in irresistible sweet reads from Jean Oram...

Read the entire Veils and Vows series!
The Promise
The Surprise Wedding
A Pinch of Commitment
The Wedding Plan
Accidentally Married
The Marriage Pledge
Mail Order Soulmate

Psst! Did you know Jean's newsletter subscribers get The Promise for free? I know! How awesome is that? So quick! Get your name on her list and get your book at www.jeanoram.com/freebook

Have you fallen in love with Blueberry Springs?
Catch up with your friends and their adventures...

Book 1: Whiskey and Gumdrops (Mandy & Frankie)
Book 2: Rum and Raindrops (Jen & Rob)
Book 3: Eggnog and Candy Canes (Katie & Nash)
Book 4: Sweet Treats (3 short stories—Mandy, Amber, & Nicola)
Book 5: Vodka and Chocolate Drops (Amber & Scott)
Book 6: Tequila and Candy Drops (Nicola & Todd)
Companion Novel: Champagne and Lemon Drops (Beth & Oz)

SUMMER SISTERS TAME THE BILLIONAIRES

Get Swept Away

Taming billionaires has never been so sweet.

The Summer Sisters Tame the Billionaires

One cottage. Four sisters. And four billionaires who will sweep them off their feet.

Love and Rumors

Love and Dreams

Love and Trust

Love and Danger

Love and Mistletoe

Jean Oram is a *New York Times* and *USA Today* bestselling romance author. Inspiration for her small town series came from her own upbringing on the Canadian prairies. Although, so far, none of her characters have grown up in an old schoolhouse or worked on a bee farm. Jean still lives on the prairie with her husband, two kids, and big shaggy dog where she can be found out playing in the snow or hiking.

Do you have questions, feedback, or just want to say hi? Connect with me:

Become an Official Fan: www.facebook.com/groups/jeanoramfans
Newsletter: www.jeanoram.com/FREEBOOK
YouTube: www.youtube.com/AuthorJeanOram
Twitter: www.twitter.com/jeanoram
Facebook: www.facebook.com/JeanOramAuthor
Website & blog: www.jeanoram.com
Email: jeanorambooks@gmail.com

73184104R00104

Made in the USA
Columbia, SC
06 July 2017